LAST CHANCE ANGEL

LAST CHANCE ANGEL

ALEX GUTTERIDGE

templar

For Michael, Chris, Nick and Emily,
with love,
and with special thanks to my editors,
Anne and Katie

A TEMPLAR BOOK

First published in the UK in 2013 by Templar Publishing,
an imprint of The Templar Company Limited,
Deepdene Lodge, Deepdene Avenue,
Dorking, Surrey, RH5 4AT, UK

www.templarco.co.uk

Copyright © 2013 by Alex Gutteridge
Cover illustration by Steven Wood

First edition

MIX
Paper from
responsible sources
FSC® C020471

ISBN 978-1-84877-299-1

Printed and bound by CPI Group (UK) Ltd, Croydon, CR0 4YY

"It is never too late to be
what you might have been."

George Eliot

SHADOWS

THURSDAY, 2 FEBRUARY – 4.15 P.M.

It was a spur of the moment decision to take the bike, one of those uncharacteristic impulses which can change your life *and* your death. We'd been given this really hard maths homework and I'd left it until the last minute. Even my brother, Jamie, couldn't work it out and he's two years older than me and went through all the GCSE stress last year. There was no point bothering Mum. She just glazes over at the mention of a fraction, and I didn't want to wait for Dad. The less I had to do with him, the better. Yasmin was my only hope.

I could have left it, but my maths teacher, Mrs Baxter, always implied that instead of being numerically challenged, I just wasn't trying. It wasn't as if I couldn't add, subtract, divide or multiply. What more do you need in life, I thought. Then she put that comment on my Christmas report card: *Jessica attends her maths lessons in body but not in spirit. It will demand a supreme effort on her behalf if she is to achieve her potential. Does she have it in her? It remains to be seen.* To be fair, she did have a point. Maths *was* my favourite subject for daydreaming. I could have got top grades in that.

Looking back, I don't know why that report card got under my skin more than any of the others. It wasn't as if it was completely different to what she normally put, but this time I felt she was writing me off, condemning me to failure, and I didn't like being underestimated. It was time to show 'She of so little faith' the error of her ways, and top of my list of New Year's resolutions was to make more of an effort in my worst subject. So on 2 February at 4.15 in the afternoon I called goodbye to Mum, quietly took the bike out of the garage and set off for Yasmin's house.

There wasn't much time. It was really important that I was back by six o'clock when Dad returned from work. I daren't leave him on his own with Mum. Jamie was upstairs but his music was turned up so loudly that he never heard anything. Perhaps that's why he played it at full blast – a deliberate blocking-out policy. Boys are infuriatingly good at that. I was the complete opposite. Our family was disintegrating by the day and I needed to log every minute detail: the rows, the silences, the tracing of tears on Mum's face. Knowing exactly what was going on was my way of preparing myself, protecting myself, which seems ironic considering what happened next.

The bike was new at Christmas and Jamie would never have let me borrow it, even if I'd grovelled. As I sneaked it out of the garage I just didn't think about lights. After all, Yasmin's house was only half a mile away and I intended to be back well before dark. I should have known that the homework would take for ever because poor Yasmin had to explain the working-out again and again. She was incredibly patient as usual but I still ended up feeling as thick as congealed custard. We both deserved a treat after all that stress so she played her latest download while we drooled over photos of mega-expensive clothes in some magazines. I was just about to leave when Yasmin's mum appeared with a plate of doughnuts. It would have been rude to refuse, so by the time I finally got outside their front door it was almost six o'clock and a fine drizzle sprayed from the sky. Dusk was thickening fast.

"See you tomorrow," Yasmin called as I swung my navy rucksack over my shoulder. "Where are your lights?"

"Forgot them."

I clocked the worried look in her eyes.

"It's not far. I'll be fine."

"Haven't you got a helmet?"

She was so cautious, so practical.

"They ruin your hair."

I ran my fingers through my straight, light-brown hair. It was so fine and lacking in body at the best of times that the last thing I wanted was to flatten it even more with a helmet.

"Better flat hair than flat you," she said.

Did I shiver? Did she have a premonition at that point? Did I? I don't think so. If I'd thought anything at all it would be that accidents happened to other people.

"Promise you'll walk?" she persisted.

I smiled and nodded. I remember thinking that

it wasn't so bad to lie, to break a promise, if you didn't utter any words out loud.

"Thanks for the help," I called. "You might turn me into a maths genius yet."

She laughed and waved back, watching me walk alongside the bike until I turned the corner at the end of her road.

As soon as I was out of sight, I eased myself onto the eye-watering boy's saddle and started to pedal out of town, along Forest Road, head down against the rain, completely unaware that my life was about to change. I checked my watch. Five minutes to six. Soon Mum would be calling vainly up the stairs for Jamie to come down and Dad would be about to park his car outside the garage.

I wondered what sort of a mood he'd be in tonight. It would depend on his plans. Perhaps he'd concoct another pretend business meeting to attend, when we all knew he was going out to meet *her*. I couldn't bear the thought of Mum shouting and crying again, like last week. She had clutched at Dad's shirt to stop him leaving the house, begged him to think about what he was doing to

11

us, his treachery shrinking her eyes into their sockets.
I had watched from the kitchen door.

That's where they say you should take shelter in
an earthquake, beneath a door frame. I'd noticed how
Dad's arms stiffened by his sides, fists clenched as if
he was trying really hard not to hit her, and I moved
forward to stand between them. I was pretty sure he
wouldn't hit me but one day, if I wasn't there, one
day when Mum was on her own, he might not be able
to stop himself from lashing out at her. That was why
I had to get home before him.

My legs pumped the pedals faster and I lifted my
bum off the seat, leaning forwards, imagining I was
on the Tour de France. A small degree of satisfaction
flowed through me as I thought how my thigh
muscles were being toned. All the cars had their
lights on now and shadows stalked me, but I was
nearly there. Just a couple more minutes and I would
have been turning into our street with its hotchpotch
of houses and neatly kept gardens. But that's not
what happened.

The car swooshed out of a side road, taking
advantage of a gap in the rush-hour traffic.

12

It obviously hadn't seen me. There wasn't time to swerve, barely time to swear. We didn't stand a chance of avoiding each other. I yanked at the brakes but the drizzle had formed an oily slick all over the tarmac. A fried egg in a non-stick pan would have had a better grip than my tyres. I slammed into the passenger door with the force of a charging rhinoceros before I started to fly. I'm pretty sure I actually somersaulted over the roof of that car. It obviously wasn't Olympic gymnast standard, but for someone who can't normally manage a forward roll without cricking their neck, it felt really impressive.

It's amazing what you have time to consider in a few seconds. There was a huge steaming dog poo on the edge of the pavement and a discarded polystyrene box in the gutter. It looked as if it contained some sort of tomato pasta, but as I got closer it could have been vomit. It's difficult to tell the difference when you're in a spin. I wondered which would be the least repulsive to land in. If I'd tried harder in gym lessons I might have had more control of where I was going, but it was too late now. At least the dog poo was fresh and it might cushion my fall slightly.

I remember worrying about my mobile phone flying out of my pocket and getting lost, and that I'd forgotten to take my library books back. I don't remember thinking that I was going to die. I suppose I expected to land, brush myself down and continue on my way like they do in cartoons. That was before I plummeted to the ground like a parcel without a parachute.

The back of my head smashed into the kerb and my lower spine tried to impress itself into a storm drain but for a few blissful seconds there wasn't any pain. I looked up at the sky. It was beautiful: indigo streaked with orange and silver. A pale moon tumbled out from behind the inky rain cloud. I didn't want to move, just to stay quite still and feel that sky. My head started to feel fuzzy.

"Focus, Jess," I said to myself. "Stay here. Don't drift away."

Certain things leaped out at me as if I was in a 3D film. A leaning beech tree stretched its bare branches over the pavement and I could just make out the little brown buds at the ends of the twiggy bits. I imagined those sticky casings splitting apart in a month's time and the fresh, lime-green leaves spilling out into the open air. Someone had nailed a bird box to the trunk of that tree and a blackbird was singing its heart out directly above me. It seemed like my own personal lullaby. I hoped all of that effort didn't make it want to poop. I closed my mouth just in case and the fuzziness intensified.

At the back of my head, where it joined the pavement, a deep thudding began to pulsate from my brain. Car doors slammed, jolting me back to reality. Exhaust fumes filled my nostrils and suddenly I felt sick. A bus went past, gawping faces pressed to the filmy windows. I prayed Will wasn't on there, looking down at me with my nose reddened by the cold and mascara smudged by the rain. My heart did a little drum roll at the thought of him. He's my brother's best friend and I adore him. He's funny and good-looking with dark brown hair that curls at the nape of his neck and a lopsided smile that always makes me blush. There was no way in a trillion light years that a guy like him would ever take any notice of a girl like me. That didn't stop me dreaming, though. One day I hoped he'd see me for the fantastic, funny, attractive person I really was instead of just Jamie's kid sister. One day, if I wished hard enough, he might just ask me out.

"Don't move, love."

A man bent over me, chasing away my dreams of Will. I licked my lips in case there was the remains of a sugar moustache from the doughnut around my mouth. I tried to smile. It felt odd, as if my head was opening up at the back. Someone was crying. How dare they! If anyone had permission to cry it should be me. I was the one in trouble, with dog poo in my hair and one favourite red Converse trainer idling in vomited pasta.

"You're going to be okay," the man said soothingly.

I'd never doubted it until that moment. I started to wonder how badly damaged the bike was and how long it would take me to save up for a replacement. Funny, I didn't wonder how badly damaged I was. A siren started up in the distance. The road hummed beneath me as cars drove past, everyone carrying on with their lives. It was comforting to know that the whole world didn't need to stop and have a look. It couldn't be that bad.

"The ambulance is coming."

The man's steady hand was warm and reassuring as it grasped my shaking one.

I tried to remember whether I'd got my best knickers on. Gran always joked that you should wear nice underwear in case you had an accident and needed to go to hospital. I had a horrible feeling that I'd let her down and was wearing the frayed, greyish ones that said Tuesday. It was Thursday, wasn't it, or was it Friday?

My eyes started to go fuzzy like a television that needs tuning and I could smell curry among the drifting exhaust smoke. I hoped it wasn't Mum's. She makes a really rank curry. Her face flickered in front of me, her fair wavy hair drifting in front of her heart-shaped face. She had freckles too and a small, snub nose. She looked young for her age, or she had done until Dad started messing about. I tried to lift my arm to check my watch. It must have been after six o'clock, and Dad would be home. I needed to be there.

17

As I tried to move, a sudden pain swerved through my head and an ice-cold feeling twined its way upwards from my toes. The road surface didn't feel so solid any more. The tarmac seemed to be softening beneath me like it did under the intense heat of last summer. Its gooey blackness was sucking me down like a vat of Gran's treacle toffee. Crashing white noise filled my ears, drowning out the blackbird. I wanted to hear that bird.

That's when I started to scrabble for breath as the fear floundered through me. Someone else was crying now, and there was pain. So much pain everywhere. The back of my head felt sticky. I wondered if I was bleeding. I can't stand the sight of blood. It makes me feel faint. The sky was so beautiful but it was getting dimmer. The crying got louder. "Shut up," I wanted to shout. "Shut up, will you! You're scaring me." Just before I lost consciousness I realised that the cries were mine.

TEMPTATION

FRIDAY, 3 MARCH – 8.30 A.M.

The journey seemed to take ages and I hadn't
been prepared. One minute I was lying in
my hospital bed, trying to hang on to everything
going on – the bleep of the monitors, Mum's voice
which was getting more and more distant – and
then there was someone calling me. It wasn't a
voice I recognised and I didn't want to listen but it
was right inside my head, calling my name again
and again. I felt as if I had a rope around my feet,
dragging me towards the entrance to a tunnel.

"Mum," I wanted to shout, "hold on to me.
Don't let me go."

But even without the horrible hospital tube
down my throat I wouldn't have been able to say
anything. For days and days I'd been trying to let
them all know that I was there, that I could hear
them. But none of them heard my cries for help,

not the doctors or nurses, not my brother or my gran, not even Mum and Dad. I was the only one who could hear the screams inside my head.

The tunnel was full of bright light and the voice that was calling me was so persuasive, as if it belonged to one of those Sirens who were supposed to lure sailors to their doom. I knew it wasn't right, that I should block my ears, but the voice twined around me like the bindweed at the bottom of Gran's garden and I couldn't help myself. I was being sucked upwards, feet first, as if there was some giant vacuum cleaner at the other end of that tunnel. I put my hands out, splayed my feet, but there was nothing to grab on to, nothing to help me slow down or stop my journey. Besides, I hadn't got much strength.

Up and up I went, looping around corners so fast that I felt dizzy, my eyes flickering against the light which was getting brighter and whiter until suddenly it was all over. I was spewed out of the tunnel and landed in a crumpled heap at someone's feet. I'd braced myself, expecting it to hurt, but there was just this white, cotton-wool softness and mist, lots of mist. The man standing next to me had a pale, angular face with arched eyebrows and a creepy lack of lines. He didn't look friendly, but it wasn't that which made me tremble. It was the shimmering gold ring above his head and the silver-tipped wings which fanned out behind his arms. Unless I was mistaken, or was hallucinating, I had landed at the feet of what looked distinctly like an angel.

The angel's beautifully manicured fingernails played a little tune as they tapped impatiently against a cloud-shaped clipboard.

"Name?"

He barely glanced at me.

"Jessica."

"Full name," he demanded. "There are a whole host of Jessicas up here."

"Jessica Rowley."

"Age?"

He stifled a yawn and I struggled to stand up. It was hard, like trying to walk in those ball pools that Mum used to take me to when I was little. I wobbled to an upright position and blinked. Where was I? What was I doing in this strange place? It must be a dream. Soon I would wake up, wouldn't I?

"I'm fourteen and…" I hesitated. I'd lost track of time. "My birthday's January the twenty-fifth."

"Aquarius," he murmured, scanning the list in front of him. "That's a bad sign."

He flicked over several sheets of impossibly thin paper and pursed his lips.

"Are you booked in?"

"I'm sorry?" I was floating now and it was the strangest sensation. I wanted to sit down, to feel something solid and secure beneath me.

"Concentrate!" He snapped his fingers right in front of my face. "I asked if you're booked in?"

"I don't know," I whispered.

I wanted to go back to the safety of the hospital bed, back to Mum holding my hand and Dad sounding falsely jolly.

"Did you pick up your ticket?"

The angel flicked a bit of his highlighted hair back into place.

"No."

He threw up his hands in apparent frustration. I wanted to cry.

22

"All the tickets for today are in a little box halfway up the Flume of Fate. I re-stocked it myself only a couple of hours ago, despite having a mountain of other things to do, I might add. You have *no* idea how long my list is…"

"I'm sorry. I must have missed them."

Why was he being like this? Couldn't he see that I wasn't well? The receptionist in my doctor's surgery was more welcoming, even if you only went in with a cold. I put up my hand as if I was in school.

"Yes? What is it?"

He sighed so hard the flowers on his very loud shirt seemed to wilt. I knew that something was terribly wrong. Why couldn't I shake myself out of this dream?

"W-what exactly is the Flume of Fate?"

"It's the fast lane to Paradise, of course. This is the processing room. You have to go through here first, having picked up your ticket with your name on it."

I was shaking quite violently now, so I wrapped my arms around myself and tried to suppress the sobs that were building inside me like a tidal wave.

"Th-there must have been some mistake. This isn't right. I shouldn't be here."

The words tumbled out, tasting of salty tears and something else – fear. I don't think I'd ever felt proper fear until then. It was like an acid waterfall crashing down on me. I felt as if I was dissolving into the surrounding mist, disappearing until there was nothing left of Jessica Rowley any more. He wafted a hand theatrically across his forehead.

"Of course you should be here. We don't make mistakes." He sighed again.

I looked around for an exit. Nothing to be seen except dense fog and this creature who had me trapped.

"You people don't make this job any easier. Even if you didn't pick up a ticket you should still be on the list."

He lifted his gaze and eyed me critically.

"You're definitely not. Are you late?"

"I don't know," I whispered. "I don't know anything – what time it is, what's happening to me…"

I swallowed, vaguely reassured by my basic bodily functions.

"I don't understand."

"That's what they all say," he replied, "or most of them, anyway. We get the odd one that's ready but most of them are quite difficult."

"Most of whom?"

Why did I say that? Why did I play into his hands? He rolled his eyes underneath perfectly curled and separated eyelashes. Another over-the-top sigh swished from deep within him.

"The Dead, of course."

When I came to I was lying on a pure white couch and he was fanning me with his clipboard.

"If I had a pound for everyone that's passed out at those words I'd be able to put in for gold-plated wings," he muttered. "Right, let's get on with this, shall we? It's nearly my going-home time."

Home – how I wanted to go home!

"It's possible you should have arrived yesterday, which was my day off, and someone's forgotten to give me a late arrival chitty."

"I don't want to be here."

I couldn't hold back the sobs any longer.

25

"No one does at first," he said, matter-of-factly, "but you'll get used to it."

"I won't. I want to go home. Please let me go home."

"You can't."

He flourished a piece of paper and a quill pen towards me.

"Fill in this form, stating at the top date of death."

I pressed my lips together, shook my head and put my hands behind my back.

"It's Friday, March the third," he said. "Eight-forty a.m."

I felt my eyes widen and my mouth fall open. March – a whole month since the accident. I couldn't believe it. I sat up and wiped my eyes with the back of my hand. What could I do? There must be something...

'The thing is," I said, "I'm not sure that I'm quite dead yet. I've been in a coma, you see, and although I can't move or open my eyes I can hear things. I know what's going on around me. I'm going to get better. I know I am."

Was it my imagination, or had a few worry lines shimmied across his forehead?

"I admit that the last I heard it wasn't good, but I don't remember anyone saying that I was…"

It was so difficult to say the word. It stuck in my throat.

"… dying."

I spat it out like a piece of mouldy apple, and he could hardly have had a worse reaction if I'd announced that I'd got a mega-dose of nits. Horror intensified the baby-blue of his eyes, his hands flew to his cheeks and he jumped back several paces. The clipboard dropped into the fog beneath his feet.

"Not another one dilly-dallying," he snapped. "How *did* you get past security? What *are* you doing here if it's not a definite demise? There's no try-before-you-buy up here, you know. I thought it was too good to be true. Everything's been totally tickety-boo all night, and then you turn up."

"Someone called me," I said. "It sounded like you."

"Maybe it was and maybe it wasn't," he replied, a little bit sulkily. "I can't remember. It's been a busy shift."

Suddenly he perked up and pushed back his shirt cuffs.

"A coma, you say. Does that mean you had an accident?"

"I was on my brother's bike."

"Lights?"

I shook my head. He jumped up and down as if he was really pleased with himself. Little particles of cloud puffed up around his knees.

"Helmet?"

"They make you look geeky."

"That hospital gown isn't exactly a fashion statement," he sneered.

"It's not my choice," I fired back. "Look, are you sure there hasn't been a mistake? I admit that I took the bike without asking, which isn't like me. Normally I'm quite sensible, but I was in a hurry. I thought I'd be home before it got dark, but the maths took longer than…"

He held up a hand to stop me. The clipboard spiralled up from the cloud and landed in his palm. He leafed through more pages. Suddenly he was very still, and I'm sure his halo slipped slightly.

"Oops," he lilted. "My fault…"

I swear my heart swelled.

"You mean I'm not going to die?"

He shot me a smile.

"Now that would be cause for concern. No, it's not as bad as that."

He pointed to a squiggle of writing.

"I've got my fives and my threes mixed up. You're not expected for another couple of days."

He glanced around as if to check whether we were being watched.

"We've got a bit of an issue here. I can't let you in before time, not without St Peter's permission."

He leaned closer and dropped his voice to a barely audible whisper.

"You'll have to go back…"

I felt a smile start to take shape inside me. Then he smashed it to pieces.

"… just until Sunday."

So there was no get-out clause after all. Tears flowed freely down my cheeks. Lying in that coma, I'd been thinking of all the things I would do when I got better but I'd been fooling myself.

Despite my prayers, I'd never be able to speak and laugh and run about again, not on earth anyway. I'd never get another chance to argue with Jamie, go into town with my friends or try flirting with Will. It didn't seem fair. I mean, I wasn't asking for an amazing life. A normal one would do.

When Gran started to sing to me last week I knew it wasn't a good sign but I'd still refused to believe the worst. Now, even *my* obstinate hope was crumbling like a biscuit at the bottom of my school bag. Much as I wanted to go back to the real world, what was the point? Another couple of days of feeling Mum and Dad shrink with grief as I faded away – it felt like too much to bear. Now that I was here I might as well stay. It's amazing how you feel differently when you've taken a decision, when you have a bit of control.

I wiped my cheeks and squared my shoulders. If this was it, THE END, then I was going to at least try to be dignified and not behave like a victim.

"You're joking," I gulped. "Haven't my family been through enough? Wouldn't it be better to get it over and done with? Besides, two more journeys in the Flume of Fate are more than anyone should have to put up with. All that bright light could give me a migraine and believe me, my head's in a pretty bad way as it is without any extra help from you. *And* I nearly had a panic attack. I've been very claustrophobic since my brother shut me in a cupboard when I was four."

I paused for breath. Had I got any breath? I must have: my voice was coming from somewhere and my chest was heaving up and down. My teeth grated against each other but I wasn't going to let nerves get the better of me now. Don't let him know how scared you are, Jess, I thought to myself, or he'll take over and you won't have any say in what happens next.

"It's freezing up here. My feet are getting frostbite. *You've* put me through this nightmare and now you won't let me through the Pearly Gates. It's not good enough."

I felt quite proud of myself. Momentarily, I seemed to have surprised him too. A look of alarm crossed his face and he took a step back.

"Where is St Peter?" I demanded. "Why can't you get his permission?"

"He's off sick with stress and can't possibly be disturbed."

Slowly, deliberately, he placed his delicate hands on his hips and jutted out his chin. I knew that stance. Mum used it when I wanted a new pair of expensive shoes or to stay out really late or to eat chocolate muffins for breakfast. Even so, I wasn't fazed.

Angel of Death: 2 , Jessica: 1, I thought. Let's see if I can level the score.

"When will St Peter be back?"

"I've no idea. January and February are such busy times for us. It's all got on top of him, the poor dear."

"This is really rubbish service," I managed to say in a more assertive voice. "*You* get the date wrong, *you* put me through that awful journey and then expect me to go back without so much as an apology. If my mum was here she wouldn't let you get away with this and nor would my gran. She knows all of her retail rights and believe me, you wouldn't want to get on the wrong side of her. She'd tell me to complain."

He didn't like that. I'd hit a nerve, if he had any. I was on a roll.

"It can't be acceptable to call people early and then

send them back. I could demand compensation. I could even contact the papers. What do you have up here, *The Daily Spirit* or something? That wouldn't be very good for business, would it?"

I paused and glared at him. I had sounded just like Mum before Dad's affair stole her self-belief. I was even intimidating myself. I watched as what little colour he had drained from his cheeks.

"Whoa! Calm down, Jessica Rowley," he flustered. "There's no need for any complaints. There must be a way to sort this out to suit both of us."

Gran says that silence can sometimes be more effective than words so I didn't reply.

"I'll get into such a lot of trouble if you report me," he said whiningly. "It'll mean a black mark on my report card. I could get demoted, and you seem like quite a nice girl. You wouldn't want that, would you?"

Actually, I would, I thought, but I didn't say it.

"So, what's the answer then?"

He looked around, stepped closer, and kept his voice low.

"I could grant you a wish – to make up for the inconvenience. I don't have the power of life over death but other things can be arranged."

"Such as?"

He shrugged.

"I don't know. It's up to you to choose. What do you want?"

I thought for a moment.

"What I really want is to see my friends. They haven't been allowed to visit me in hospital. I don't know why – probably because I've been so ill. Even my best friend, Sara, hasn't been to see me. Mum says that she's been phoning every couple of days, though, to find out how I am. Apparently everyone at school is praying for me in assembly. I really want to see Sara. I need to know that she's okay. Then there's Yas – I don't want her to feel too bad about the accident. And Kelly's hoping to be picked for the county tennis team but she's got such a lot on her plate already, without having me to worry about. And Nat—"

He held up a hand.

"Stop! How many of these friends are there?"

"Just one more, just Nat. I *have* to tell you about her."

His wings sagged a little.

"Go on then," he said.

"Nat's not seemed herself recently," I said. "Before I had the accident she'd lost quite a lot of weight. I mean, she's always been careful about her figure but, well, I'm worried she might be taking it a bit far this time."

I bit my lip and studied my hands before looking up at him.

"If I'm going to die…"

"You are," he interrupted.

I frowned and he looked slightly apologetic.

"*If* I'm going to die," I repeated, "I need to see my friends before I go. They've been the best group of friends I could have wished for. I want to say goodbye."

I could see alarm registering on his face.

"Okay," I said. "I can see that might be a bit difficult. It was stupid of me to ask."

"Not at all," he said. "I can do that – sort of."

I frowned.

"What do you mean, 'sort of'?"

"Well, you'd be totally invisible, so you could see them but they wouldn't be able to see you. I think an invisible Jessica Rowley talking to them might be a bit scary, don't you? You could watch and listen to them, though."

There was an evil glint in his eye.

"You might even find out what they really think of you and discover a few secrets about them too. It could be interesting."

"We don't have any secrets from each other."

He threw back his head and laughed. It wasn't a nice sound.

"Mock all you like," I flared, "but we don't."

"Whatever." He grinned, studying a calendar which had suddenly materialised through the mist. "So, are we going for this invisible visit, or what?"

"How long have I got?" I asked.

"You're due back on the fifth but I can change the five into an eight. If anyone asks any awkward questions I can always say it's to give us a bit of time to catch up with the winter backlog. I'll send you back first class," he added. "It'll make the journey more bearable."

"What do I have to do?"

"Oh, absolutely nothing," he replied. "I'll send you directly to the hospital bed, and when you're ready you can slip your spirit out of your body and off you go. Easy-peasy."

Finally, I looked straight into the clearest, brightest blue eyes I had ever seen.

"How do I know that I won't be whisked straight back up here, without a moment's notice?"

"You have my word – as long as you stick to the rules."

"What rules?"

"You must just visit your friends, no one else. You mustn't have contact with family or pets or anyone…"

He winced slightly.

"… anyone close. That would be extremely undesirable."

"If you say so," I muttered.

"I do."

He held out his hand. Tentatively, I shook it. It was cool and surprisingly firm. His palm felt as soft as goosedown.

"What's your name?" I asked.

"I'm Darren, an angel of death dedicated to your service."

He gave a small bow. As I went to pull my hand away he clasped my wrist and leaned towards me. His grip was like a vice.

"You *must* return. I want you back in your hospital bed and ready for collection on Wednesday the eighth at one minute past midnight. If I can slip you in at the start of the day it'll be a bit easier."

"Fine," I said, shrugging.

His eyes hardened.

"I have the horrible feeling that I'm being a complete idiot here. You will remember what I said? You will remember the rules?"

He was having doubts, thinking of changing his mind. I could sense it. Keep your tone light, Jess, I thought, or he'll never let you go. He'll keep you up here shackled in some foggy corner until the time is right.

"Of course. Don't worry. I'll do as I'm told and I'll be there on the eighth."

He stared at me. I wanted to look away but knew that I mustn't. My brief future depended upon it. I managed a weak smile.

"I promise."

He paused and released my wrist, clicking the fingers of his other hand.

A silver surfboard appeared in front of me and I lay down on it. To the side of him the fog cleared, revealing the entrance to the tunnel.

"You've got five days, Jessica Rowley," he said, and the slightest push with his foot was all it took to send me careering back to the real world.

FREEDOM

FRIDAY, 3 MARCH – 8.59 A.M.

The return journey passed in a flash and I was back in my body just as if I'd never been away. I wondered if there'd be a bit of a panic, or if someone might have noticed something different, but nothing seemed to have changed. I was aware of Mum hunched by the bed in almost the same pose as I left her in. The first few nights after the accident she'd slept in the chair next to me. Now she went home, but she obviously didn't sleep properly because sometimes she was back really early, before the rest of the world woke up.

It seemed as if I'd been away for ages, yet it had probably only been a few minutes at most. I was acutely aware of everything – the starchiness of the sheets, the banging of doors in the distance, the clunking of the machines, the scent of the primroses on the table at the end of the bed. Every couple of days Mum picked them from the border outside the kitchen window at home and brought them in to show me.

"Here we are, Jess," she'd say. "Aren't they lovely?"

She'd waft the flowers under my nostrils, completely unaware of how their subtle scent tugged at my heartstrings. One spring, when I was very small, I'd snapped off every single one of the tender yellow heads with my still-clumsy, babyish fingers. Mum was so cross but Dad was my protector then. He'd understood that I couldn't resist them because they were so pretty. He was the one who had fished the wilting flower heads out of the bin and floated them in a blue glass bowl brimming with water.

It was one of those silly family stories that got repeated every year. If it was February it was the primrose story, and it got so predictable and boring and, if Will was around, embarrassing. But now I longed to sit at the kitchen table with a resigned expression on my face while Dad teased Mum for getting so cross and Jamie reminded me of the time

I'd screamed when I found a worm in my pocket. Everyone would laugh, even me in the end, despite the fact that I still can't bear worms.

Now, after a month in that hospital bed, I almost couldn't remember what laughter sounded like. Instead, my ears were tormented by the sound of Mum's heart breaking. It didn't seem possible for it to shatter into any more pieces, and I knew that even time spent in her beloved garden would never be able to totally heal the damage.

It was stupid to wait when I had so little time. The clock was ticking down the minutes and there were four special people to see. The thought of getting away was tantalising but I was scared to actually try it. What if it didn't work? What if it did? Surely they would notice if I got up from the bed and walked? I lay there all morning, waiting for a break in 'Jessica watch', berating myself for wasting the precious time I could have with my friends.

At last there was a lull in the patrol. Mum was going home for a rest and Dad had come back from work to take over. They walked to the window and I heard Mum rummaging about in her handbag.

I foresaw Dad talking me through the whole ninety minutes of the previous night's England versus Holland football match. As it had ended in a nil–nil draw and I'd already heard the radio commentary, I decided it was worth risking a break-out.

Sliding my spirit out of my damaged body was easier than I thought. Neither Mum nor Dad paid any attention as I sat on the edge of the bed and stretched my arms and legs. Although I was barely visible, even to myself, I was relieved that I still appeared to be wearing the gown and wasn't completely naked. Only the edges of my body seemed to be defined, like the wispiest waft of steam from a kettle. In the middle, I was nothing apart from a slight pulsating at the centre of my chest, where my heart should have been. Seeing that made me feel a bit strange.

"Get a grip, Jess," I said to myself. "This is you, not some gruesome experiment in biology, and this may be your last ever chance to hang out with everyone you love."

The locker at the side of my bed was crowded with cards – even Mrs Baxter had sent one –

but in pride of place was the card from my friends. Yasmin had drawn it herself and she'd included all my favourite things on the front. In the middle was Samantha, my guinea pig, with a big speech bubble coming out of her mouth in which Yas had written 'Get Well Soon' in lashings of pink glitter. Encircling Samantha were turquoise dolphins, nose to tail, and around the edge was a border of shoes. At each of the four corners was a sprig of cherry blossom and inside the card Sara, Kelly, Nat and Yas had written their own special messages. Mum had read them out to me and described the pictures. Knowing the card was there, just to the side of my poor battered head, was one of the things that kept me going when I got desperate, but finally being able to see it for myself was awesome.

"Thanks guys," I mouthed. "It's so beautiful and I love all of you too."

I half floated, half swam towards the door, hanging on to the frame so that I could turn and look back at myself lying in the bed. I looked horrendous. It wasn't the colour of my skin or the fact that I'd lost weight. It wasn't the drip in my arm or the tube down my throat. It wasn't even the fact that they'd had to shave part of my hair when they dealt with my smashed skull. In fact, if you ignored all those things, I probably didn't look that bad to anyone who didn't know me. To strangers I might have just looked as if I was asleep, but to me there was an emptiness. I was like one of those waxwork figures in Madame Tussaud's. There was no sign of all those invisible bits which made up my character, my sense of humour, my impatience, my longing for fairness and loyalty, my stubbornness. Without being able to show all of those qualities, good and bad, which I took for granted, I was nothing, no one, just a husk. How creepy was that?

At least I understood why all the doctors and nurses kept prodding me, shining a light in my eyes and asking me silly questions in dopey voices. I also understood why they sounded as if they weren't expecting me to answer. Mum, Dad, Gran and Jamie seemed to have drawn up a rota to carry on where the doctors and nurses left off. They'd spent the last month talking to me about anything and everything. It was as if words were the kisses that would make everything better and they felt that I wouldn't slip away while they were still talking. I shivered, and my whole invisible form rippled like a raindrop chasing its way down a pane of glass. Any day now, any minute, the doctors might persuade them that I wasn't worth keeping alive and the machine which was helping me to breath would be switched off. Is that what would happen? Is that how Darren the Angel of Death would finally get me?

Dad crossed the room and settled down in the chair closest to my inert body. He took my hand in both of his. As he bent over I could see how his hair had thinned and the skin was sagging around his chin. He looked older. A flickering hope lit up my brain – perhaps the other woman wouldn't be so keen on him now. Mum made for the door and I grabbed the frame, propelling myself out of the way, hoping to slip out of the room alongside her. She turned to look back at me lying in the bed.

"Something's wrong."

The room resonated with her fear.

"Nothing's wrong," Dad soothed. He pointed to the monitors. "There's no change."

Mum frowned. Her skin was tinged with grey and she'd lost loads of weight. We must be nearly the same size now, I thought. She'd be able to fit into my clothes if she wanted to. Maybe when I was no longer around she would use some of them. That new pale blue jumper which I hadn't even had the chance to wear would probably suit her.

"Jessica Rowley, you're in a very negative mood today." Mrs Baxter's voice permeated my thoughts.

Whoa! That was scary. Where had she come from? Why had my brain conjured her up now? Was I going mad?

"You are the sum of your thoughts, Jessica."

There it was again, her direct, uncompromising voice, irritatingly reverberating from the centre of my head, saying the words she'd said to me over and over again in maths lessons. "If you think you can't, you can't. Whereas if you think you can…"

"Think you can what?" I snapped back.

"Live, of course," she replied.

"Yeah, right," I answered sarcastically, "and I'll be in Set 1 for maths by next Christmas as well."

47

"Anything's possible…" she began.

"Not this," I replied, shaking my head to try and get rid of the vision of her face which had suddenly, scarily appeared before my eyes.

"Will you go away!" I instructed. "I've got things to be getting on with and I don't need any distractions."

She pursed her lips, and gave me one of those looks that made me feel as if I wasn't trying hard enough.

"Face it, Mrs B," I said. "I know that you don't like to be proved wrong, but even with your help I'm not going to get out of this mess."

She shrugged.

"Maybe you're right, Jess. After all, no one's right all the time, are they?" She paused. "Not even an angel."

And she disappeared, but she left her words with me. Somewhere, deep in my befuddled brain, a pinprick of hope emerged. Was it possible that I could escape my fate?

"I felt something," Mum gulped. "Don't you think she looks a bit different?"

That pulsating in my chest quickened as they studied my shell.

"It looks as though part of her is missing," Mum sobbed.

Dad stood up and took her in his arms.

"You're imagining it," he murmured, stroking her hair.

I'd forgotten what it was like to see them have a hug. "Don't let him touch you," I wanted to shout at Mum. "He's had those arms around her. He's betrayed us." But, at the same time, Mum needed someone to lean on and I was grateful to see them holding each other close. After a couple of minutes she pulled away and wiped her eyes. They kissed, the tiniest touch of lips, before she reached for the door handle, and we left the room together.

I couldn't believe that no one could see me so I kept close to the wall, like Samantha, my guinea pig, when she's set free in my bedroom. I'd been so worried about her, convinced that Jamie would forget to feed her or give her fresh water and she'd be pining to death in her cage. Then there was my diary. If Jamie actually remembered his guinea pig duties, would he rummage around for my diary when he was in my room? Would he read it and would he show it to Mum or even Dad? There were some pages I would have quite liked Dad to see, to make him realise how much he had hurt me, but I definitely didn't want Jamie reading the bits about Will, or Mum finding out that I'd got three detentions at school for forgetting to hand in homework. She thought I'd had to stay late because I needed to look something up in the library. Thank goodness parents are so easily fooled.

Mum wasn't walking fast but I couldn't keep up with her.

"Wait for me, Mum," I wanted to call as she disappeared into the distance.

I tried to speed up, but it was hopeless. I was floating rather than walking and it was all happening in slow motion. The night before the accident I had painted my toenails in Posh Petunia, and as I looked down at my feet I could just make out the barest hint of ten pink toes winking back. I'd managed to connect my feet with the floor but I couldn't feel the coldness of the lino and I had to use all my energy to do a sort of drunken forward walk. To the left, a doctor flung open a door, the slight draught blowing me sideways.

"Oh, for goodness' sake," I grumbled. "This is ridiculous. Doomladen Darren might have mentioned how hard this was going to be. If I don't get better control of my movements than this it's going to take me days just to get out of the hospital."

A swarm of nurses bustled down the corridor and I flattened myself against the wall before sinking onto a low window sill. I felt exhausted. I'd never be able to get around town in this state. I'd never make it to my friends' houses. I might as well admit defeat and drift back to bed. My bum was sandwiched between a vase of fake yellow chrysanthemums and a picture frame containing a prayer.

Two floors down there was a little courtyard garden with benches and clipped lavender bushes edging the gravel paths. It was totally surrounded by hospital walls but it looked so enticing.

"Concentrate, Jessica," I said to myself in my best Mrs Baxterish voice. "You don't know what you're capable of until you really try. You can go out there, and once again breathe disinfectant-free air."

I stood up, and instead of trying to walk began to glide as if I were on ice. I'd never been much of a skater, but surprisingly it worked. I was moving at a reasonable pace *and* in the right direction.

"Ouch!" I stubbed my toe on one of those stupid rubber bungs they use to stop doors banging back against the wall. I expected it to hurt, but the pain was minuscule and probably more a result of anxiety about chipping the Posh Petunia polish, if that was possible. Can you chip something that isn't really there? I didn't know, but those feet were the only things about me that felt half decent and I wanted to keep them that way.

At the end of the corridor was a geriatric ward, and under a chair by the door I spotted a pair of really uncool slippers. The next-door bed was stripped of its sheets and it took only seconds to convince myself that the slippers had been left behind when the occupant had 'moved on'. Briefly, I wondered if that person had had the misfortune to meet 'my friend' Darren or if there were other Angels of Death doing the rounds.

The sheepskin-lined bootees immediately became

invisible as I squeezed my feet into them. It was like magic, and I stifled a giggle. I'd forgotten what that felt like. It was like drinking a whole bottle of lemonade and feeling all the bubbles burst inside you.

A porter sailed past, whistling softly and pushing an elderly lady on a trolley. I was feeling braver now and I did a little leap, landing right on the end of the trolley, totally amazed by the fact that the sheet didn't even ruffle. The porter wheeled us into the lift and pushed the button for the ground floor. I clasped my hands together. I felt as if I was fizzing with excitement. I had done it. I was on my way back to the world, back to freedom and, best of all, back to see my friends for one last time.

HOME

FRIDAY, 3 MARCH – 12.09 P.M.

In the foyer I had to wait for someone heavier than me to activate the automatic doors. Then as soon as I shimmied out of the hospital, the north-east wind blasted me in the face.

"Wow! That's strong," I gasped, lunging towards a porch pillar and clinging to it for dear life. "This could be a bit of a problem," I murmured. "I could be blown all over the place, maybe across the Channel."

We *were* an awfully long way from the sea, but it was possible, wasn't it? I could have been like one of those balloons they release for charity that are found hundreds of miles from home. When Darren had offered me this opportunity to slip out of my body and be invisible, I'd never thought it would be so difficult.

"Challenging, dear," Mrs Baxter's voice drilled

into my head. "It's not difficult, it's just challenging. You need to change your perspective. Think about it in a different way."

"Not you again," I muttered. "Give me a break, will you?"

I clung to my pillar and looked around me. From the way people were dressed, the wind was obviously bitingly cold. Everyone was wrapped up as if on an Arctic expedition, but I was wearing a hospital gown which was open down the back and all I felt was a slight tingling, like one of those peppermint face masks that make you feel as if you don't fit properly into your own skin.

At least I didn't feel half dead any more. A couple of unchopped tendrils of hair blew across my eyes and I wanted to laugh out loud just because I was here, in the real world, but I daren't. Even though people couldn't see me, they might be able to hear me; that was something I still had to put to the test, but now wasn't the time. Now it was more important that I worked out how to use this wind to my advantage.

A covered walkway led to the main road and

people had their heads down, bracing themselves as their coats billowed out behind them. There was no way I was going to be strong enough to fight my way through that wind tunnel.

"Think, Jess, think," I instructed.

And there it was, my solution. It wasn't ideal. It would take more time, which was something I was painfully short of, but it was the only option. I would have to go the long way around, and there was no time to waste.

"Here we go," I said, releasing the pillar. A mischievous current of air caught me up and whisked me straight round to the back of the hospital. At first I was tumbling and spinning all over the place, trying to hold the gown down and preserve my modesty. Once I relaxed a little, unclamped my arms from my sides and spread them out to my sides to help me to balance better, it was brilliant. I felt as if I was flying like a rather ungainly bird that had been trapped in a cage for too long. I stretched out my fingers, pointed my toes and turned my face up to the pale blue sky. I was outside, away from the thick airlessness of the hospital room and, at that moment, it was the best feeling in the whole world. Even the traffic's humming and buzzing sounded like my own personal welcome-back-to-the-world song.

It was as if I'd been away for a long holiday and was seeing everything from a new perspective. The trees were coming into leaf and everything looked brighter and more beautiful than I remembered. A horrible thought suddenly grabbed me. I got homesick just being away from home for a couple of days; heaven only knew how I would manage an eternity. I wondered what would happen if I didn't return to that carcass still lying in the hospital bed. Would Darren really bother to come and find me when he was under so much pressure?

There was a sudden lull in the wind and I dropped down to earth, just on the other side of the safety barrier to the car park. As I looked towards the road I could see Mum's car waiting at the traffic lights. I wanted those lights to stick on red so that I could run over and dive into the front seat. When I'd been lying in bed, waiting to make my escape, I knew where it was that I wanted to go straight away – to see Sara. She was my best and oldest friend so she had to come first. But standing there, watching Mum's Ford Fiesta turn the corner and head towards home, I changed my mind. It wasn't part of the deal, but I had to go back and see my bedroom. I had to check on Samantha, look at all my precious possessions and maybe get out of the hospital gown. Until I'd done that, I couldn't concentrate on anything else, and Darren would never know, would he?

Buses stopped right outside the hospital, but not the one I wanted. My bus, the number 29, went from the front of the train station and the best way to get there was straight up the new road past the rugby ground. Normally that would be a fifteen-minute walk at most. As I lurked by the traffic lights, the wind tried desperately to whip my gown up around my face and wrench my feet from under me. The small, newly planted saplings in the middle of the carriageway looked as if they were also struggling to stay tethered to the ground. My flying skills were still pretty non-existent and it's difficult to keep your decency when you've got to flap your arms out to the side to keep your balance. Besides, I just didn't want to risk being blown away for miles in the wrong direction or propelled underneath the wheels of a lorry, so I opted to try to walk.

Taking the longer route, I was protected by the towering red-brick prison walls and kinder, narrower streets. Nearly an hour later I stumbled over the pedestrian crossing and could have hugged the driver when I found my bus already waiting.

It felt really sneaky slipping on board without paying, but it wasn't as if space was limited. Upstairs was completely empty and I collapsed into the seats right at the front. Sara, Nat, Kelly, Yas and I always raced to sit there. We liked to dodge the overhanging branches as they smacked into the window. Last time we'd done that Nat had got a bit carried away and screamed as she threw herself into the aisle, knocking into some elderly lady's shopping bag. Half a dozen oranges rolled to the back of the bus like bowling balls. We'd got some really dirty looks, but we all had tears of laughter streaming down our cheeks as we crawled around trying to retrieve the fruit.

Thinking about that made me want to cry, sad tears this time. In my normal human form I cried easily, at the slightest excuse, but now my eyes were bone dry. I propped my feet against the front of the bus and looked out of the window. We lumbered up Forest Road past the park where my brother plays football on a Saturday morning and on past the church where my parents got married and Jamie and I were christened.

"That's where my funeral will be, I suppose," I murmured, and a shudder ran through me.

The bus slowly circled the prettiest roundabout in town; it brimmed with miniature daffodils and bright purple aubretia. Then we were almost there, at the place where it had happened. A lump formed in my throat. What if there were flowers to mark the spot? That would be a sign, wouldn't it – a sign that I was really dead and that all of this was just some horrible trick.

I didn't want to look but I couldn't help myself. My head may have been fixed straight ahead but my eyeballs slid to the side and stared at the spot. A sigh of relief rippled through me. There wasn't a clue as to what had occurred, no inkling that Death lurked on that cosy-looking corner with its neat hedges and bewitching bursts of spring.

I buried my head in my hands, the relief dissolving faster than an ice cube held under the hot tap. If only I hadn't been in such a hurry, if only Dad wasn't having an affair, if only I wasn't so stupid and the maths hadn't taken so long, if only I had left earlier, if only I hadn't broken my promise to Yasmin about walking, if only it hadn't been raining I might have been able to stop in time, if only I'd had lights. So many 'if onlys'.

I had worked myself up into such a state that I nearly missed my stop but I hit the bell at the last minute, forcing the driver to brake sharply. I gripped the top of the rail with both hands, swivelled down the stairs without making a sound and dashed out of the open doors. As I stood on the pavement looking back, the driver was shaking his head, totally bemused. The sight of him made me smile.

My house has lovely large sash windows and a friendly red front door. The porch floor is covered with black and white Edwardian tiles which look really smart next to the crimson paint. It's a tall house but it doesn't bear down on you. Instead, it looks like the sort of house that wants to wrap its walls around you and give you a big hug. Someone had planted up the wicker hanging basket with giant yellow pansies, and snuggled around the drainpipe that reaches up past the landing window little pink clematis flowers were blooming.

I'd never noticed before how pretty everything was. It felt as if I'd been away for months, not just a few weeks, and I couldn't wait to get inside. I tried the shiny brass door handle and vaguely wondered when Mum was finding time to get out the duster and polish. The door was locked, of course, as was the side gate, and I had no idea what had happened to my keys after the accident. My foot-stamping was worthy of a two-year-old and my whole body rippled like a stone-splashed pool. Wishy-washy shades of blue shimmered from my gown and momentarily I looked like the background sky to one of those delicate watercolours Gran paints at her art class. Seconds later I had faded back to a ghostly mistiness.

"Now use that brain, Jessica."

I pretended to peer over my spectacles like Mrs Baxter.

"What do ghosts do, dear?"

"They walk through walls," I replied. "At least that's what they do in films, and this whole situation is fantastic enough to be a film."

There was a lavender bush next to the porch and I pinched a couple of leaves between my fingers, lifting them up to my nose. My nostrils detected the faintest smell but I was sure that it should have been stronger, that it was me at fault and not the lavender. People say that ghosts sometimes have a distinctive aroma. I decided there and then that if I was going to come back and do any haunting I would like to smell like lavender. It's one of my favourite scents.

As I wasn't officially a ghost yet but just on the waiting list, I decided a bit of training wouldn't go amiss. First of all I leaned gently against the front door and tried to melt into it. Nothing happened. There was obviously a knack to this and I wasn't getting it right.

"Perhaps a big run-up is needed," I muttered.

I modelled myself on Will, who's a fast bowler and looks really irresistible in his cricket whites. Big mistake. Vaporising through woodwork was obviously something else to add to my list of things to improve upon. In my human form I'd probably have dislocated my shoulder as I slammed my whole self into the solid panelling before slumping down on to the doormat, but all I felt was a slight ache. I didn't think I'd made much of a noise – the slightest rattle of the letter box, maybe – but inside the house I heard meticulous footsteps crossing the parquet floor. I just managed to crawl across the gravel out of her way before Gran stepped onto the path and scanned the street.

"What are you doing here, Gran?" I murmured. "I thought you'd be at your house."

She was wearing some dangly silver earrings I had bought her for Christmas and a severe expression on her face. I longed to reach up and stroke those nipped-in cheeks and to bury my face in her pink cashmere cardigan but I couldn't risk it. She might have a heart attack, and being responsible for my own demise was more than enough to cope with, let alone having Gran's death on my conscience. I stood up and tiptoed towards the door. Thankfully I was so unusually light-footed that the gravel didn't crunch at all. I didn't even make any indentations. Gran sighed, shook her head and bent to pick up the milk carrier. As I slipped past, I brushed the back of her skirt and she stood to attention faster than one of the guards outside Buckingham Palace.

"Who's there?" she asked, spinning around.

If only I could have told her not to worry, that it was only me. It was unbearable. I just fluttered upstairs to my bedroom and floated down onto my flowery duvet. I felt absolutely exhausted, but it was so good to be back, surrounded by all my precious things.

The room looked almost the same as when I had left it: a little tidier, maybe, without the usual half-finished mugs of tea on my bedside table and the clothes piled on the back of my chair. The guinea pig cage was in its usual place, though, on top of my chest of drawers. There wasn't a sound from inside the little blue igloo where Samantha sleeps, and the pulsating from my heart space seemed to stop. I *was* almost dead already though so that probably didn't matter. I crept over the carpet and peered inside. Blackcurrant eyes gleamed in the shadow but she was so still. Perhaps she'd died and nobody had realised. Then she squeaked. It was absolutely one of the best sounds in the whole world.

"Oh Sammy," I gasped. "You know that I'm here, don't you?"

"Squeak, squeak, squeak," she replied.

"Shh!" I put my finger to my lips. "You'll have Gran up here wondering what's going on."

I fumbled with the door to the cage and scratched between her ears with my clumsy fingers. She threw back her head and squeaked again.

"Okay, okay," I said. "I'll try to pick you up, but don't blame me if I drop you."

It was easier than I thought. She was completely still as I lifted her between my hands and I could feel the slightest warmth in my palms from her little tummy.

"I can sort of feel you, Sammy," I said, plucking her from the cage and cuddling her to me, "but everything's a bit numb, as if I've had a bad case of pins and needles. But I am so happy to see you."

I sat on the bed and placed her gently on my lap. To anyone else she'd have looked as if she was sitting on the duvet but I knew she wasn't. I could just feel her claws against my legs and her nose nudging my fingers. I lay back against the pillow as she scrabbled over me, seemingly oblivious to the fact that I wasn't 'all there'. She felt as light and feathery as I did myself as she tickled my chin and nibbled at my gown.

"Have they been feeding you enough?" I asked, putting my hands around her tummy. "Hmm, guess you haven't been off your food and pining for me then?"

I lifted Sam down onto the floor so that she could have a run around and opened my wardrobe. If at all possible, the gown had to go, but I wasn't sure what would happen if I changed my clothes. I prayed they'd become invisible like the granny slippers. I felt like a personal shopper as I scrutinised every garment, trying to decide what would make me look and feel better.

Several things were obviously going to be too

big, especially the grey striped shorts, and I'd gone off the black dress with the rose print. I wanted to wear something bright and cheerful, so in the end I chose an emerald green sweatshirt and some red jeans which had actually been a bit on the tight side when I bought them. Gran always says 'red and green should never be seen' but I think that's one of those old-fashioned sayings that don't apply any more. Besides, the trousers were perhaps more coral than red and the cut of them made my legs look longer. I'd had the sweatshirt for ages but it was still one of my favourites, and the green enhanced my eyes. I rummaged inside my chest of drawers for some underwear and took off the gown. It became visible the second it left my body.

"Uh-oh! I'm going to have to find somewhere to hide that," I muttered and stuffed it at the back of the wardrobe underneath a collection of handbags.

Thankfully, as soon as I put on my own clothes they disappeared into thin air. In *my* eyes I did look a little brighter, but as I stood back and examined myself in the mirror I was convinced that no one else would be able to see me. Over the next few days, as I got closer to death, I wondered if my faint iridescence would fade away like a dissolving rainbow. That's probably what would have happened in a film. Maybe, eventually, I would no longer be able to see myself at all. I pressed my hands against my cheeks. How scary would that be, when even I hadn't the slightest visible sign that I still existed?

"Stop it, Jess," I instructed. "There's no point thinking about that now."

I did a little twirl right in front of the guinea pig.

"Considering I'm at death's door, Sammie, I don't look too bad at all, do I?"

She stopped her exploration for a moment and stuck her nose in the air as if in agreement. It made me feel a whole lot better.

Carefully, I brushed the remains of my hair and pulled on some socks before studying footwear options. The shocking pink Doc Martens, which had been a Christmas present from Mum and Dad, didn't really go with the rest of what I was wearing but they'd barely had a chance to come out of the box. They were begging for an outing and it cut me to the core that I had to resist. The other clothes probably wouldn't be missed if Mum went rooting around, but if those boots disappeared from my wardrobe serious questions might be asked. I chose some old pink trainers which Dad had been on at me to throw away but I couldn't bear to get rid of just because they were faded and frayed.

I sat on the floor to fumble with laces and glanced under my bed. It was where I kept my diary. My stomach jolted. It wasn't there. I prowled the room in a state of panic, opening my bedside cupboard, my dressing table drawers, floating up a little less easily now to look on top of the wardrobe. I found the diary in my bookshelves, slotted between my horoscope book and a small hardback about the meaning of dreams. I grabbed it and sank to the floor, turning it over in my hands, searching for signs that Mum, Dad or Jamie had been trawling through my private thoughts, but there weren't any dog-eared pages or greasy thumb prints. It looked exactly as I had left it. Sam scuttled over and started to chew the bottom of the bookshelf. I gathered her in my arms and held her little face up to mine.

"It doesn't matter if they have found out all my secrets, does it, Sam? I won't be here to get the lecture from Mum about school or the ribbing from Jamie about Will anyway."

Despair felt as if it was making a gaping hole behind my breastbone.

"I don't want to die, Sammie. I want to live, even if it does mean being teased and told off and everyone seeing into my soul."

I placed Sam back on the floor and lay down beside her, curling up in a ball on the raspberry-coloured carpet. Lying there, like that, I felt safe from harm.

"I haven't written a will, Sam," I said. "People of my age don't do that sort of thing, do they? But perhaps they ought to. I should have thought about what would happen to you if I wasn't here. I suppose Mum and Dad will look after you. Jamie might even move you into his room. I'd like that, and I'd like him to use my savings to feed you on organic vegetables and buy you one of those super-duper guinea pig palaces. I definitely want Sara to have my gold locket. She could put two photos inside it, one of her and one of me, and then we'd be together forever. Yasmin ought to have my books. She'd give them a good home, and Nat's always liked the silk sarong with the dolphin print that Gran and Gramps brought back from Australia."

I was wondering whether to give Kelly my favourite teddy bear or the Beatrix Potter ornament collection, when the bedroom door opened. Gran stood on the threshold in her stockinged feet, which must be why I didn't hear her coming up the stairs. I lay completely still as she scanned the room with those eyes that normally don't miss a thing. The diary lay open in the middle of the carpet and Sam was in the process of weeing on my best cartoon drawing of Mrs Baxter. Gran stared at the guinea pig for a moment before pulling the door to. I sat up and heard a click as she picked up the phone in my parents' bedroom. There was a pause as she waited for the person at the other end to answer.

"I need to speak to Mr Rowley, please. He should be there, visiting Jessica."

My bedroom door didn't catch properly unless you gave it a good tug so it was very slightly ajar.

I padded over so that I could hear a bit better.

"Andrew!" Her voice was all ratchety. "Is everything all right?"

I imagined Dad's curt reply. He and Gran never really got on, even before the other woman came on the scene.

"It's just that I went into Jess's room and the guinea pig is loose and…" Her voice sounded all shaky. "Something didn't seem quite right. I can't explain it, just a feeling. You're sure there hasn't been any change?"

I leaned against the wall and looked to where Sam had scuttled under the dressing table.

"What do I do now?" I mouthed at her. "Do I put you back and pretend it never happened, in which case Gran will probably think she's going senile, or do I leave you to cause havoc?"

A car door slammed outside my window and I took a flying leap over the bed to see Mum's car parked outside the gate. She was unloading a couple of bags of vegetables from the back seat and I could hear Gran scooting down the stairs, sounding as if she was barely picking her feet up on the way. I tut-tutted with my tongue. She was always telling me to walk properly or I'd wear out the carpet, but then I suppose these days threadbare stairs were the least of everyone's worries.

Mum was accosted the minute she walked into the hall and within seconds there were two sets of footsteps racing up the stairs. Sam had never liked anyone picking her up other than me, and I stood on the bed half grimacing, half smiling, as Gran and Mum tried to catch one very disgruntled guinea pig.

"I can't understand it," Mum said, lunging towards a corner. "Jamie gives her a cuddle and a brush every morning before school, but he's always very careful to put her back."

I stifled a laugh as Sam darted straight through Gran's hands while my mouth dropped open at the thought of my brother taking the trouble to groom my guinea pig. It was nice, though, to think of him holding her and giving her some love. I sent him a silent message over the airwaves.

"Thanks, Jamie. Wish you were here, but I guess you've gone to see me straight from school."

Jamie's visits to the hospital had been my link to normality. He told me the things I wanted to hear, the important things like which celebrities had split up, gossip from school and the occasional get-well message from Will.

"Hiya, Jess," Jamie would call, even before he reached my bed.

I'd listen for the thud as he dropped his school bag in some inconvenient place and then I'd brace myself for THE KISS. Yuk! Who wants to be kissed by their brother? He'd never kissed me before, so why now? I knew it wasn't a good sign. There was a plus side, though. He'd always picked up something to eat on the bus so sometimes I got a blast of bacon or cheeseburger and chips or, my own personal favourite, chicken tikka ciabatta. They were real-life smells and made me feel sad and jealous and hopeful all at the same time. My brother's stomach is a bottomless pit, even in a time of crisis, and as soon as he'd made himself comfortable in the chair next to my bed I would hear the rustle of chocolate wrappers and the crunch of crisps, and savour a delicious waft of coffee. I became convinced he was doing it on purpose, to torment me.

Often, he didn't stay long at the hospital and after a while his voice would sound husky, as if he'd been smoking, but I knew he hadn't. When you can't see you learn to listen, to feel, to smell. Just because your eyes won't open it doesn't mean you don't know what's going on. When my brother brushed his hand against mine as I lay in that hospital bed, I felt the roughness of his cuticles, I heard the little chewing noises he made as he bit them to the quick, I sensed the tension in his shoulders and heard the faintest sound as he ran desperate fingers through his hair. I didn't like it when he got upset. He was the one I relied upon to give me a boost, and I realised that I wanted him here now, in my bedroom, to dilute the sadness which seemed to cling to Mum and Gran.

"There's the diary as well," Gran said, a little breathlessly. She was on her hands and knees now, reaching underneath my dressing table for the third time.

"Got you!" she exclaimed triumphantly, holding Sam a safe distance away from her appetising jumper, before placing her back in the cage.

Mum picked up the diary and dabbed the wee-adorned page with a tissue.

"I think I'll keep it somewhere safe," she said, and there was the faintest catch in her voice, a blink of a pause, "until Jess comes home."

"Oh Mum," I wanted to shout. "I'm so, so sorry, but I'm not coming back. At least that's what I've been told. Haven't you been told that too? Isn't that why the doctor took you into that side room the other day – to tell you that there's not much hope?"

"There's always hope, Jessica."

There she was again, Mrs Baxter, fixing her opinions to me as annoyingly as those sticky labels that won't ever come off, even when you soak things in hot water.

"No, there isn't," I replied. "Why won't you accept that I'm hopeless at maths? And even if I could think of a way to get out of this life versus death problem, I'd probably be hopeless at that too."

Suddenly I couldn't bear to be in that room for a moment longer. I couldn't bear to stay in my house, with all the reminders of the things and people I loved.

"Sorry, Sam. I've got to go but I'll be back. I promise," I whispered.

I blew her a kiss, jumped off the bed and stumbled to the top of the stairs. I launched myself from the top step and flew through the air, landing with a soft but distinctive thud at the bottom. I heard it, and Gran and Mum must have heard it too. I looked up to see them peering over the banisters, a look of alarm on both their faces. Mum hadn't closed the front door properly and I flailed towards the opening as if I was swimming a very bad front crawl.

At the end of the garden path I pulled up and leaned against the gatepost. By then Mum and Gran were downstairs, standing on the porch step, looking towards the road. For one stupid moment I thought they could see me – that they had actually watched me go.

WARNING

"If they could see you they'd have called out," I said to myself as I half walked, half floated down the street. "They'd have tried to stop you leaving. No one can see you, Jessica. No one knows that you're wandering about in this limbo land. You're all alone. Cry. Go on, cry. Feel sorry for yourself, and let those tears form puddles on the pavement."

It was no good. Try as I might, my eyes were still as dry as the Sahara desert. At the T-junction at the bottom of the road I had no idea which way to turn. Where was I going? What was I going to do next? My mind was in a complete whirl, so when someone called my name I just about jumped out of my stupid invisible body.

"Jessica Rowley! This really isn't good enough. I should have known you were trouble."

He was perched on top of the post box, sitting like one of those fairy ornaments which Gran has in her garden, except he wasn't wearing a friendly fairy face. Darren the Angel of Death looked cross, very cross indeed.

"Don't do that," I gasped, clutching my hands to my throat. "People can die of shock, you know."

He smirked.

"Of course I do. Unfortunately, it's quite a long way down the Expiry List and I haven't been allowed to try it out yet. The other more experienced angels get all the fun."

"The others?" I queried. "You mean there's more than one angel of death?"

"Oh yes," he said, stretching out his long legs and hopping down on to the pavement next to me. "There are hordes of us. We're all at different levels."

He bit his lip as if he'd said something he regretted.

"And what level are you?"

"That's not something you need to know."

I narrowed my eyes.

"Are you even qualified?"

He placed the back of his hand against his forehead

and staggered backwards.

"What an insinuation!" he gasped. "I'll have you know I'm very highly thought of. My family have been doing this for generations. Now, back to the business in hand."

My legs began to wobble and I clutched the post box for support.

"Y-you haven't come to take me away, have you? I've only had a few hours. We've got an agreement."

"Precisely," he replied, waggling a finger in front of my face. "Rules, Jessica Rowley! You're not obeying the rules. That's why I'm here. I clearly stated that you could visit your friends. I specifically told you not to go home. Did I say you could have a cuddle with the undeniably gorgeous guinea pig? No! In fact, I said that you were to steer well clear of anything which might tug at your heartstrings."

I started to speak but he held up a hand.

"There are reasons for these rules, Jessica Rowley, and the main one is to make my angelic life and your human death easier for both of us.

If you continue to go off-message then it's not going to work and I shall have to start getting tough."

He paused.

"We don't want that, do we? If you don't obey the rules you might get some silly idea that your demise could be avoided. And believe me, that's not going to happen."

He laughed. It was a mean, grating laugh, and a flock of pigeons scattered from the tree above me.

"I know that," I whispered. "I only came home to change my clothes. I'm sorry. You said yourself that the hospital gown wasn't a good look."

He looked me up and down.

"Nice jeans, but hasn't anyone ever told you about colour co-ordination? You look like a rather gaudy Christmas tree."

"I wanted to wear something cheerful," I snapped. "I wanted to feel more like myself for the next few days. Besides," I carried on, staring at his shirt, "you're not so subdued yourself."

He leaned back, an expression of mock horror on his face.

"Dear me, we are touchy, aren't we? The thing

is, Jessica Rowley, I don't want to be forced into dragging you back kicking and screaming because you haven't followed my instructions and you've gone and re-attached yourself, like a limpet, to the rock of life."

"I won't," I replied. "You've made it quite clear that there's no hope."

"I'm glad we understand each other."

"So you won't take me away just yet?"

He tilted his head and pursed his lips. The silver tips of his wings glinted in the sunlight. I curled my fingers and felt my nails digging into the palms of my hands.

"I could be making a huge mistake here," he said, placing his index finger against his chin. "The most sensible thing would be to take you back with me now and hide you in some cloud-filled cupboard until Judgement Day. I really don't know why I didn't think of that before."

"No!" I almost shouted, and he looked startled. "No," I said more softly. "You're not making a mistake. I promise. I won't let you down."

"And you won't go back *there* again?" He flicked

83

his golden hair towards the top of the road, towards home. "Promise?"

"I promise."

There was a lump in my throat and the slightest prickling behind my eyes.

"All right," he said, checking his watch. "Now, if we've got this sorted out I must be off."

He leaped back up onto the post box and stretched out his wings. I shivered in their shadow.

"Darren," I asked as he stood on tiptoe, "how did you know I was here? Have you been following me since I left the hospital?"

"Goodness me," he protested. "I'm not a babysitter. I haven't got time to watch over you all the time."

I frowned.

"Then how…"

He threw his hands in the air.

"So many questions. Do you always ask this many questions? Your teachers must have found you an absolute nightmare. If you must know, it's a tingling in the wings, a hissing of the halo, that lets me know when something isn't right. You have to be good, Jessica Rowley, or I'll be back, and next time

I may not be so nice. Remember the rules. It's your friends you're meant to be seeing."

I nodded, and a gust of air blasted into me as he took off, soaring upwards into the distance. I landed on my back and lay looking up as, with a final flourish of his hand, he drew the word 'friends' in loops of light across the sky.

"Point taken," I murmured, picking myself up. "Come on, Jessica. That's what you're here for, so let's get going."

SARA

FRIDAY, 3 MARCH – 4.56 P.M.

I had to visit Sara first, not just because her house is the closest to mine but because we'd been best friends for so long. On our first day at nursery school she'd pulled one of my plaits and I'd cried. The next day she offered me her biscuit, and that was it – we clicked. Who can resist someone who offers them a biscuit, especially if it's chocolate malted milk?

Some of the teachers used to get us mixed up or think we were sisters because we look a bit alike with our smattering of freckles and greyish green eyes. I wish! If we were related I might have her brains and that great smile which draws everyone in. I used to think that Sara was brave and confident and together, all the things I wanted to be. I used to think that she could handle anything with grace and humour but now I know differently.

Before the accident, I thought that Sara was the

only person who knew how I really felt about Will. I could tell her anything and she never laughed at me for worrying about silly things which might never happen or made light of bigger problems. She knew all about my family issues too and her house was one of my escapes.

"If you ever need to get away for a while, Jess," she said, when Dad started messing about with the other woman, "then come to my house. Any time of the day or night, it doesn't matter. You're always welcome."

I hugged her when she said that. I wanted to hug her mum, too, because she never made me feel as if I was in the way and she always asked if I wanted to stay for supper, even when there probably wasn't enough food to stretch to one extra person.

When Sara's mum talked, I noticed how her dad paid really close attention, nodding and smiling and watching her all the time. It was as if they'd only just met and he didn't want to miss a single word she said to anyone. He didn't get that distant look in his eyes like my dad.

There was nearly always laughter in that house. It bounced off the walls, making the atmosphere all bubbly and happy. Most of the time I loved being there, but sometimes all that happiness was just too much to take. It reminded me of how close we used to be as a family, and Sara understood that I had to get away from her house too. Not that she's perfect, far from it. She used to get really irritated with her little brothers, especially when they went into her room and started messing around with her things. Then the fireworks would start and it was better for me to keep a low profile. She may look all peaches-and-cream calm on the surface but she's got an impatient, temperamental streak, and when she wants something, she's pretty determined.

On the whole, though, I loved spending time there. I almost felt like one of the family and I often told Sara how lucky she was to be part of it. Looking back, I'm not really sure that she truly appreciated how precious normal life can be. It wasn't her fault. I realise now that most people don't, until they've had it taken away from them. Until your life starts to go wrong you take loads of things for granted.

By the time I'd manoeuvred my invisible body around to Sara's house it was about five o'clock. Her dad had obviously finished work early as his car was already parked outside. I peered through the bay window at the front and could see the boys sprawled across the sofa watching a DVD. There was no sign of Sara and a horrible thought turned my aura a sort of battleship grey. It was a Friday night and the five of us often got together. What if Sara had already gone out? Would one of the gang have stepped into my size four shoes and taken over organising what we were going to do, when and where?

I supposed it would have to happen eventually, when I was no longer around, but it seemed a bit presumptuous for them to be cutting me out already. I wasn't particularly organised in other areas of my life, and sorting out all that social stuff hadn't come naturally at first, but everyone else had seemed happy for me to take charge. So it was usually me who organised a trip to the cinema or bowling alley or suggested staying in to make our own pizzas and watch a rom-com.

"You're so good at it," Nat had said when I suggested someone else might like to take over.

"I can do it if you want," Yasmin offered, "but it wouldn't work nearly as well."

"You just seem to know when we need to stay in and chill and when we need to go out," Kelly added.

Sara had put her arm around me.

"We love you sorting us out and telling us what to do," she'd said.

"You mean I'm bossy," I replied.

"Yeah!" she laughed and pinched the top of my arm, "but where would we be without you, bossy boots? We'd all be billy no-mates, buried in our books! We love you for it."

"And I love you too, guys," I murmured as I skirted the side of Sara's house. "I may be at death's door and will never get the chance to organise a trip to the movies again, but please, please don't have taken this job off me before I've actually totally gone from your lives."

I sidled down the passage, past the bins and towards the kitchen at the back of the house.

"Sara," I murmured, "I really need to see you. Please be here."

90

I looked up at her bedroom window and floated across the lawn to get a better view. I hoped to see the lamp lit up on her window sill but the room was in darkness. Holding on to the washing line, I blew about, letting myself swing upwards like the clumsiest gymnast in the world. My aim was to fly up through the air so that I could catch a glimpse of the top of Sara's head as she sat on her bed, looking at her laptop. It didn't work, and I didn't dare let go of the line in case I was wafted away, over the top of the house and carried somewhere I really didn't want to go. Anyway, it didn't really matter that the lamp was switched off or that I couldn't see into the room properly because I knew Sara wasn't there. I could feel it, just as I could feel a sort of desperation welling up inside me. As I fluttered down to earth and sank onto the grass, the back door opened and Sara's mum threw some bread onto the lawn for the birds.

"What about the crispy duck?" she called over her shoulder. "You know that's your favourite."

I wanted to cheer. It was just what I wanted to hear. Crispy duck was always what Sara chose when

91

I went to her house and we had a Chinese takeaway.

"She's here, she's here," I sang to myself, and I did a silly little dance around a rose bed.

The trouble was, all that rejoicing meant I missed my opportunity to get into the house. By the time I had floundered across the patio it was too late and her mum had slammed the door in my face. I edged sideways and pressed my face to the window. Sara was slouched on one of the pine kitchen chairs, running her long, slim fingers around the rim of a mug.

"Hi! It's me."

I waved through the window. I knew it was stupid, that she wouldn't have the faintest idea I was there, but I couldn't help myself.

She looked really pale and she'd obviously been working overtime with the straighteners.

Her hair was normally a bit wavy but now it was even straighter than mine *and* she was biting her nails. Sara never bit her nails. She just looked so different, not like my bubbly Sara at all. I *had* to get in there, to see her properly, to hear her voice. Dissolving through doors was obviously out of the question so I wondered about trying to squeeze myself through the cat flap. My hospital stay might have contributed to a flatter stomach but my hips looked pretty much the same. The last thing I wanted was to get stuck halfway through the flap and be at the mercy of Fluffy, the most evil cat in the world. That cat catches everything that moves: squirrels, birds, frogs – they all end up dead under Sara's bed. If Fluffy sensed I was there and picked up the scent of guinea pig, she could shred me to smithereens in seconds.

The cat flap dropped to the bottom of my mental list while I considered shinning up the drainpipe and trying to slide in through the open bathroom window, but that didn't seem a much better idea. I wasn't very good with heights and as this was my first day of freedom it seemed foolish to take unnecessary risks and maybe hurt myself.

"Patience, Jessica dear," Mrs Baxter's voice droned in my ear. "You're always in such a hurry."

"But I haven't got much time," I fretted and dropped my head into my hands. As if to add to my fears, the nearby church clock chimed half past five.

In the end, I didn't have to wait long. Sara's dad headed out for the takeaway half an hour later. I made a complete mess of my first attempt to get inside the house, nearly getting trapped in the door and sliced in half, but by the time he came back, loaded with polystyrene boxes, I was prepared.

At last I stood in the hall and I felt rather pleased with myself. It was so good to stand on those wide golden oak floorboards, looking at Sara's school blazer draped over the banisters at the bottom of the stairs. While they sorted out their food, I tried to soak up the atmosphere, to take some sort of strength from being inside the house, but I felt confused. Something was different. The atmosphere was heavy and the voices coming from the kitchen were muted. When everyone took their loaded plates through to the sitting room I joined them, slipping through the half-open door and hovering near the fish tank.

"Don't you just love Fridays?" Sara's dad said, as he sank into the chair near the fireplace and picked up his fork.

I nodded. Friday evenings used to be my favourite time too – no school for two whole days and the

94

weekend stretching ahead – but Sara's Mum glared at him. An awkward silence filled the room. Sara let her hair fall forwards around her face and picked at her crispy duck with her fingers. Even the boys were subdued, spooning egg fried rice into their mouths without their usual chatter.

"So, how about getting the bikes out tomorrow?" Sara's mum suggested, after what seemed like hours but was only five minutes and twenty-three seconds later according to the clock on the mantelpiece. "There isn't any rain forecast. Sara, what do you think? The fresh air would do you good. You've been spending too much time cooped up inside."

"There's something I'd rather do," she replied quietly, "if you'll let me."

Suddenly the room bulged with tension. I could feel it squashing me from all sides, as if I was being sealed into a tight airless package.

"I saw Jamie on the way back from school," Sara carried on, not waiting for anyone to ask what it was she wanted to do. Presumably they already knew and they weren't at all keen. "He thinks it might help if Jess has some visitors."

95

I went to clap my hands and just managed to stop myself in time.

"Yes, please," I mouthed. "That's exactly what I want."

"She's got visitors," her mum shot back, the words darting across the room as fast as one of those little rainbow fish in the tank next to me. "She's got her family."

"But Jamie thinks it must be a bit boring for her," Sara persisted, "listening to the same people talk all the time."

Yep! I nodded. He's right there. I hadn't realised my brother was so perceptive. I was beginning to see him in a whole new light.

"I really don't think he should have put you in that position," her mother retorted. "It's not on. You know what we've agreed."

Sara dumped her plate down by her feet.

"He didn't actually ask me to go, so there's no need to lay into him, but I *need* to see her." Her voice was getting quite shrill. "I don't understand why you won't let me. Surely anything's worth a try and it just might help to bring her back to us, mightn't it?"

"Yes, yes it might," I wanted to shout out loud.

"Sara, sweetheart," her father said in a solemn voice, "you know we've talked about this a thousand times. It would be very upsetting for you to see Jess at the moment and we just can't bear that."

"Jess's parents agree with us," Sara's mother added in an instant. "They think it would be too distressing for you as well."

Sara stood up, her cheeks flared with colour.

"I'm not four years old. I can cope. Why don't you understand it's just as distressing for me *not* to see her? She's my best friend. What will she be thinking, lying there, knowing that I haven't been to visit?"

I watched as Sara's parents threw each other knowing glances. You didn't need to be a mind-reader to know that they thought I was a hopeless case, that I wasn't aware of anything as I lay in that hospital bed.

"She'll think I don't care about her," Sara carried on.

She was crying now, tears coursing down her cheeks, her hands flailing about as if they were being manipulated by some manic puppeteer.

No! No! My whole body rippled in protest. I don't think that. I've never really thought that… not for long anyway.

It was so hard to stop myself from going over and consoling her. I put my hands up against my cheeks as I watched her father shove his plate onto the coffee table and leap from his seat to put his arms around her.

"You see," he said, with a touch of triumph, "this is just what we're trying to avoid: any more upset."

"You *don't* understand," Sara shouted, pulling away, hair stuck to her tear-stained face. "However many times I tell you, you don't understand that you're making it worse."

She sent her cutlery flying as she stormed across the room. The knife hit the skirting board, chipping the paintwork, but Sara didn't care. She was already out of the door and taking the stairs two at a time.

I don't quite know how I managed it but I was with her in an instant, close on her heels, caught up in her slipstream. As she went to slam the bedroom door behind her, I put out my hands to stop it closing.

She turned around with an exasperated huff and came back a second time to make sure it shut. In the meantime I was in her room, pressed against the 'Keep Calm and Carry On' poster which I'd given her for Christmas. She flung herself onto the bed and sobbed so hard that the blue upholstered headboard banged against the wall. I wanted to put my arm on the centre of her back, to tell her it was okay, that I understood now, that I'd always known she'd never let me down, but I couldn't do anything. I felt completely useless.

It wasn't meant to be like this. While I'd been lying in the hospital bed, waiting for my chance to get away, I'd imagined how we'd spend our last precious time together. Sara would have been sitting on the floor pinning up her hair or maybe doing some sewing. She was really good at making things – cushions, perfect patchwork cases to keep your phone or camera in. I'd have sat next to her, watching her select pieces of fabric from the box at the bottom of her bed, before she placed them on the floor, working out which patterns and colours looked best next to each other. Instead, I sank onto the beanbag and covered my ears with my hands, willing her to stop crying, wishing her mum or dad would come upstairs to comfort her, but no one did.

In the end, she dried her eyes. I expected her to spend some time on Facebook with Nat and Yas but instead she did start to sew. She was making a cushion from hexagonal pieces in different shades of blue and she sat at the sewing machine in the corner of her room, listening to her iPod and joining the fabric together with a zigag stitch of navy cotton. The whirr of the machine was soothing and I'd almost dropped off to sleep when there was a noise outside the door. Sara must have a sixth sense because she got up, took out her earphones, crossed the room and opened the door.

Uh-oh! I thought. Here comes trouble.

"Oh Fluffs," Sara said, bending down to pick up the cat. "In you come."

As she dipped her forehead and laid it lightly in between Fluffy's ears, I wondered whether I should make a break for it. Too late! Those sage-green feline eyes locked on to mine and I felt a faint tingling sensation down my spine as I saw the cat flex her claws.

"What's the matter, Fluffs?" Sara asked, tickling Fluffy under her chin. "You missing Jess too?"

Ha! Ha! Very funny. I almost laughed out loud.

As Sara put Fluffy down on the bed I braced myself, waiting for the cat to pounce, but instead, much to my surprise, she began to purr.

"I'm making a cushion for Jess," Sara continued, "for when she wakes up. Do you think she'll like it?"

My throat felt all tight. I bit my lip.

"I've got to get on with it, Fluffs, because she could wake up any time. It could be tonight or tomorrow morning. It could be in the next five minutes even, but whenever it is, I want this to be ready for when I see her again. It's going to be the best cushion I've ever made."

She was sort of smiling now, trying to look brave. It just about broke me in two. I really wanted to be able to cry. I wanted those tears to flow and my nose to run. I wanted to thump the floor and say how sorry I was for taking the bike, for never properly telling her what a great friend she was. We used to say that as soon as our parents would allow it we'd go on holiday together, and then later on, after school, take a gap year. We used to say that if we didn't get married we'd probably end up sharing a house when we were old and grey. She'd have about six cats and I would rescue guinea pigs. None of that would happen now – not with me, anyway. Fluffy jumped on to Sara's knee.

"They will let me go and see Jess when she wakes up, won't they, Fluffs?" she asked, snipping at a piece of cotton. "And if they won't, I'll go anyway. As soon as Jamie says she's awake, I'll be there, helping her to get better. You too, Fluffs. You must be nice to Jess when she comes around to the house. No more arching your back and hissing at her. I can love both of you at the same time, you know. If you just give her a chance, Jess will learn to love you too. I know she will. You may have scratched her a couple of times but she's not the sort of person to bear a grudge."

Sara's eyes were bright with tears again.

"I'll never have another best friend like Jess, Fluffy. Never, not in my whole life. You know that, don't you?"

"And I'll never have a best friend like you, Sara,"

I whispered.

I'd planned to spend the night in her room, not to sleep – time was too short for that – but just to curl up on that beanbag, safe and warm. Now I couldn't stay. I couldn't sit in that room and think of all the things we'd done together, all the things we'd never get to do, so I took the coward's way out. When Sara buried her face in the cat's soft white coat I scrambled off the beanbag and made for the door. I paused and looked back at them both.

"Look after her for me, Fluffy," I whispered.

The cat lifted her head and rested her chin on Sara's forearm. Those almond-shaped eyes blinked several times. Before, I'd not been totally sure if she could see me, but in that instant I knew that she could, and I knew that in her own catlike way she was letting me know that she'd do her best.

PROBLEMS

FRIDAY, 3 MARCH – 9.01 P.M.

I tiptoed down the stairs and struggled with the front door latch. I still couldn't feel my fingers very well and the little brass catch was stiff. From the sitting room I could hear the sound of the television and occasional laughter. I wanted to storm in there and tell Sara's parents how miserable they were making her. I wanted to tell them how much it would help me to have her at my bedside for even a few minutes. But I couldn't do any of that because I wasn't sure they'd even be able to hear me, and if they could, would they be brave enough to listen to some disembodied voice and do what I asked?

I'll never know because I just didn't have the courage to even try it. Instead, after several attempts, I got the front door open and stumbled into the cool dark, night.

I'd never liked the dark. It used to make me

feel as if I was suffocating, which was why Mum always left the landing light on at home. There was a lamp post outside Sara's house and I clung to it, bathing in the pool of yellow light, unable to think straight. What could I do now? Where could I spend the night?

"Think, Jessica. Use that brain of yours," Mrs Baxter used to say.

I pressed my palms together as tightly as I could, wishing I could feel something other than this strange squidginess. It felt as if I was made up of the hand gel that hangs in a container at the end of my hospital bed. Maybe there *was* the slightest feeling of firmness beginning to creep into my lower limbs, or was it just my mind playing tricks?

I stayed very still, wrapped around the lamp post like a toddler clinging to her mother's legs. I felt totally alone, as if I was the only person left in the whole universe. No one knew where I was, not the real me anyway. They thought that shell of a person in the hospital bed was me, but it wasn't. I was here, pressing my cheek against the dirty metal lamp post and waiting for inspiration, waiting for the hopelessness, which had smothered me alongside the darkness, to disappear.

Eventually it did, and choices began to form a disorderly queue in my head. There were so many of them that I started to feel dizzy. I could do anything, go anywhere. I had the ultimate freedom. Four weeks ago if I'd been offered the chance to go somewhere new, to board a plane to the Bahamas or occupy a penthouse suite in the poshest hotel in the world, I'd have grabbed it. It's strange how quickly you can change. Now, all I craved was the comfort of things, people and places that I already knew.

I considered my options:

1. Return to the hospital bed. Definitely not. Too dangerous. Might never be able to leave again.
2. Go home. Tempting but too upsetting and against Dictator Darren's rules. Maybe later in the week I'd risk it when I'd seen Kelly and Nat and Yas but, for now, it wasn't worth taking the chance. Somehow *he* would know and I'd probably be whisked straight back 'up there' to await my fate.

3. Sneak into a hotel and try to get access to one of the rooms, preferably a luxury one. Appealing but not that easy in practice, and I'd probably end up sleeping on a sofa in the foyer. I didn't fancy that but at least it was a possibility, if I got desperate.

"If you can't decide what to do, walk it through." Gran's voice resonated in my brain like a mantra.

"I would if I could," I muttered, "but I can't walk properly at the moment, Gran. Not sure if it will work with floating but I'll give it a go."

Except that when I let go of the lamp post something strange happened. I didn't float away and my feet *were* making contact with the ground. I couldn't feel the tarmac beneath the soles of my trainers but I could see that I was standing on the pavement. I put one foot in front of the other. I was frustratingly unsteady and unsure of myself.

"For goodness' sake," I said to my body. "I was only just getting the hang of floating and now you go and do this to me. What's going on?"

Secretly, though, I felt quite pleased. Even if

107

I did look like a toddler taking her first steps, I didn't care. Walking made me feel a bit more normal… a bit more human.

At the end of Sara's street I automatically turned left, away from home, and joined the main road heading out of town. Cars sped past, headlights shining straight into my eyes, slipstream tugging at my hair. Everything seemed so different in the dark – noisier, smellier, less friendly. The air felt slightly chilly and I wished that I'd had time to grab a hat and coat before I left home in such a hurry. My stomach felt tight, as if I'd been laced into one of those Victorian corsets we'd tried on during our school visit to the costume museum last term.

As soon as possible I escaped the traffic and took the side roads. I walked and walked, occasionally stopping to study the vivid stained-glass windows of some of the houses, listen to owls having a conversation or to run my fingers over the smooth bark of a silver birch tree. I absorbed all of these things, gifts which I had barely noticed before, and they helped me to feel more comfortable with myself and the darkness.

I walked straight past the Tennis Club where Kelly plays twice a week and took the narrow path which cuts through to the church. On one side a scrubby patch of grass borders a shallow brook and I've always thought that the sound of water plinking over the pebbles sounds like someone playing a miniature xylophone.

There was a group of lads huddled together on the little bridge, taking it in turns to puff pathetically on one cigarette. Normally I'd have felt apprehensive in case they called out or – worse – decided to follow me, but I hate smoking. It killed my gramps. Instead of shrinking into myself and hoping not to be noticed, I just walked up to them, on a mission and brave as could be. I whisked the cigarette out from between the skinny one's lips and tossed it into the brook. I'd planned to walk on as if nothing had happened but as they stood around, open-mouthed, it seemed like a good opportunity to test my vocal cords.

"Hasn't anyone told you that smoking is really bad for you?" I said, and the words seemed to be swallowed up by the darkness.

They looked from one to another and then all around.

"Who said that?" one of them asked.

So they had heard me. I might have been invisible but I had a voice. It felt like another sign that I was still more than just some silly spirit.

"They put 'Smoking Kills' on the side of the packet for a reason, you know." I felt my throat area contract as I forced my voice to be louder.

"Who's that? Who's there?" the skinny one asked, trying to be all brave, but I could see a muscle twitching in the side of his neck.

"Someone who knows that you should show a bit more respect for life. As my gran says, you're a long time dead."

That spooked them.

"Let's get out of here," said the one in the baseball cap, and they scarpered up the road like a load of panic-stricken chickens.

I chuckled as I carried on walking along the path, past where a small copse cast its shadows and something foraged about in the undergrowth. Courage isn't a straight line. It can dip away from you in an instant and I felt uneasy again.

Dealing with people didn't seem too difficult, but animals were a different matter. If Sam and Fluffy were anything to go by, animals could see me, or at least sense me, so I hurried towards the play park where Mum and Dad used to take us when we were small. It's totally enclosed by high privet hedges and I felt a bit safer there. Dotted around the patch of grass are a small slide, some swings and those wooden animals on big coily springs. By the time he was about seven Jamie would pretend that he was too grown up for the little park, but I loved it. He always came out of his sulk in the end and threw himself head first down the slide or jumped on to the wooden horse and pretended he was riding the winner in the Grand National.

I hadn't realised that this was where my heart was leading me, but I was so glad to be here with all of its happy memories. I sank onto one of the swings and gently rocked myself to and fro.

"If I had another chance," I murmured, "I would never try to blot out my past. I'd never feel embarrassed about secretly playing with dolls after all my friends had shoved them in a cupboard and I would never hide in a hoodie when I went to the cinema with Mum or pretend that I'd got something else arranged when Gran suggested we went out for tea together."

At that moment I would have given almost anything to have been able to do those things again.

My legs definitely felt heavier and more solid from the walking. I used them like a giant pendulum and found myself gaining speed, swinging higher, feeling the chill on my face as the night air rushed past. My fingers were still quite numb so I gripped the chains tightly enough to give me blisters.

"Go on, Jess! Go for it! You've never been brave enough before and you'll never get the chance again."

I felt a lump in my throat, a pitter-patter in my heart space as I propelled that swing up towards the sky until there was no going back. I threw back my head, pointed my toes and allowed the momentum to carry me up towards the stars. For a split second there was just me and the sweep of space before gravity tugged me right over the top and down the other side.

"Yes!" I called to the world. "I did it. I did it."

For one fleeting moment my amazement at my new-found bravery blocked out everything else. I forgot about the accident and all the things I was going to miss. There was no past, no future, just now. It felt good.

The swing slowed and each weakening lurch brought me back down to earth. In the space of a few seconds I travelled from euphoria to the depths of despair. I fell onto my knees and crawled over to a bench in the corner. Now I knew what Gran meant when she talked about people having the life knocked out of them. Ninety-eight per cent of me wanted to slump on to those shabby wooden slats with their peeling paint and give up. What was the point of all this? Having a few extra days and being allowed to see my friends wasn't going to change anything, and it was all so shattering. My eyelids felt heavy. I still wanted to say goodbye but I hadn't been prepared for how tired all of this would make me feel.

"Don't close your eyes," I ordered. "Stay awake. You'll regret it if you don't see this through. There isn't enough time left to sleep."

Deep down I was scared to sleep, scared of never waking up again. I needed to stay awake for every second of every minute of every hour. I wanted to count every blade of grass, listen to every single sound echoing in the distance and smell each and every spring flower in more gardens than I could imagine, but I couldn't fight the feeling of tiredness any more. It was overpowering. I lay down, curled up into a ball and slept.

LEARNING

SATURDAY, 4 MARCH – 1.15 A.M.

The church clock chimes every quarter of an hour, but I didn't hear it. Even the unidentifiable creatures that scrabble and scratch in the bottom of hedges didn't disturb me. I was in a deep, dreamless sleep – until someone sat on me. I might have been invisible but I could still be squashed, and it was just my luck to get the only tramp in the world who needs to enrol at Fat Camp.

"Oi! Get off! Why don't you look what you're doing?"

I didn't think, just spoke as loudly as my wavery, disembodied voice would allow. I sounded like someone else, like someone really old. The man leaped up faster than if he'd sat on an ant hill. So did I. As well as being stocky, he was also extremely smelly and certainly seemed to have shocked my olfactory nerves back into action. Everything you ever needed to assault your senses was there – alcohol, B.O., unclean clothes and that fragrance of the moment, dustbin breath. He tried to dent the darkness by staring frantically into it. His eyes were like those almighty gobstoppers my brother buys after he's played a game of football.

"Who's there?" he slurred.

I was tempted to leg it but couldn't resist testing my vocal cords again. I glanced up at the church, the clock face just visible through the trees. The hands hovered at one-fifteen.

"Do you know what time it is?" I demanded. "My name's Jessica and I was asleep."

His response was to whirl around and claw at the night with rough, wrinkly hands.

"Where are you?" he gasped, staggering towards me.

I backed away.

"You shouldn't be wandering around at this time of night, frightening people." I replied.

After being at the mercy of everyone else for weeks it was rather nice to have the upper hand, and my voice was beginning to sound a bit better.

I could recognise it as me.

"I've been very ill. The last thing I need in my condition is a nasty shock. Besides, you could have cracked one of my ribs if I had any. You need to cut down on the carbs."

I pressed my hands gently to my thorax. Was it my imagination or did that area where my ribs should have been feel achey?

"I can't see you. You're scaring *me*."

His eyes were wide and wild, his breath rasping. Panic poured from his mouth, rushing towards me on highly flammable halitosis. The wind was getting up again and it threw a punch at the tramp's back, almost knocking him off his feet. He pawed in front of him, grasping at thin air, trying to stay grounded. I knew that feeling, so why was I being so mean to him? That wasn't like me, and I felt thoroughly ashamed of myself. There was a danger in this power. It could easily go to my head and Gran wouldn't like that – or Gramps.

"You don't want to get above yourself," he used to say, if someone had said something pompous or showy-offy. So, holding my nose with one hand,

I grabbed the tramp's arm with the other and led him back to the bench. He was too bewildered to resist.

"It's okay. You can sleep here," I said. "It's sheltered from the wind. I'll find somewhere else to go."

At the gate I turned and looked back. He'd taken a bottle out of his pocket and was unscrewing the top. I sighed and walked back towards him. He paused, the bottle half-raised to his lips.

"It may blot out the pain," I said softly, "but it does all sorts of funny things to your brain. Someone in my class drank half a bottle of neat vodka once and had to be rushed to hospital with alcohol poisoning."

"Who *are* you?" he asked again, peering into the gloom.

"Jessica," I replied, reaching out and grasping the bottle. His gnarled hand clamped itself over my invisible one.

"You've had enough. You're going to feel terrible tomorrow."

Gradually his grip slackened.

"F-feel terrible now," he slurred.

"Sleep it off," I said, reaching out and touching his shoulder.

"Are you my g-guardian angel?" he whispered.

"Something like that," I replied, and he let me take the bottle.

"That's nice," he mumbled, lying down on the bench. "I need one of those."

"Don't we all," I murmured.

He closed his eyes.

"Sleep tight," I said softly. "Everything will seem better in the morning. That's what my gran says and she's usually right."

"Sh-she must be a good person, your gran," he murmured.

"She is," I replied, but he couldn't hear me. He was already asleep, the rumble of a snore falling from his mouth and rippling through the little park.

I walked up the road and poured the vodka down a drain.

"Maybe some good has come out of my return after all," I murmured. "I think I could get quite used to being a guardian angel and helping people. It makes you feel good. Gran, you would be proud of me."

'Do something nice for someone else every

day,' was one of Gran's favourite bits of advice and she'd often dole it out if Jamie or I were having a moan about something stupid.

"Well, Gran," I murmured, dropping the empty bottle into the overflowing bin outside the newsagent's, "I've taken your advice. I've done a good deed and given my bench to someone who needs it but it has left me with a bit of a problem. Where am I going to spend the night?"

They say you need to hear someone's name mentioned three times before it registers in your brain. I felt so stupid. Of course, I knew where I could go. Why hadn't I thought of it before? If I didn't actually meet up with Gran, surely Darren wouldn't mind too much?

The little wooden gate that led into Gran's back garden had dropped on its hinges and I barely had the strength to lift it up and push it open. A fox lapped from the pond. It looked up warily as I padded across the cobbled path but it didn't run away. The small Victorian house was in total darkness and I had no idea whether Gran was here or if she was staying over at my house. My instincts told me that she was upstairs, asleep. She might have been spending the days with Mum, Dad and Jamie but, knowing Gran, she'd want to be tucked up in her own bed at night.

I wrapped my fingers around the cedar frame of the greenhouse door and slid it open. Warm air and a heady geranium scent wafted over me. It was like stepping out of a cold air-conditioned plane into a welcoming Mediterranean resort. The moon obligingly emerged from behind a cloud as I stumbled towards the old wicker chair which Gran sat in to prick out her seedlings. When I was little I used to love to help her, but a couple of years ago, when Gramps died, things changed. I didn't want to go and mess about with plants any more. Gran said she understood, that I was growing up and I was busy. She said that we couldn't expect things to stay the same for ever.

As I sank into that chair I realised that I'd abandoned her just when she needed me most. It wasn't deliberate, but it was thoughtless, which seemed almost as bad. Now I longed to stand beside her and to get soft compost under my nails once again and tenderly nurture some baby snapdragons until they were ready to plant out, but it was too late.

"Sorry, Gran," I whispered. "I really wish I could make it up to you."

Tears pooled under my eyelids and I wilted into the chair like an over-watered plant. My body complained at the lumpy cushion. I shifted and shuffled to try to get comfy before realising that my physical sensations were growing stronger. I was almost crying. My fingers were tingling and the rest of my body felt heavier. It was so strange. If anything, I'd expected to feel weaker, floatier, less and less human. Instead, I was like a baby on a journey of discovery, learning what I could and couldn't do. I was beginning to love my invisible body. In a strange sort of way it made me feel free. I didn't have to fret about the size of my thighs or the way one ear stuck out more than the other. Instead, just to be there, to be able to smell, touch and feel, was like the most wonderful present in the world. I vowed never again to complain about my straight hair or curly toes and, as if on cue, the grass snake which lives in the corner of Gran's greenhouse slithered across the end of my foot.

"Hello, grass snake," I whispered. "How lovely to feel you." And I really meant it. "I hope you don't mind me sharing your home for the night but I haven't got anywhere else to go and I am so, so tired."

I yawned. I couldn't stop my eyes from closing. Even the other creepy-crawlies that might be sharing my chair didn't bother me. For the time being I felt safe – safe enough to enjoy a tiny nap.

When I awoke, something was wrong. It was the light. It wasn't that ruthless, early morning light that makes your spots look like the plague. It had a forgiving tinge, a sort of lunchtime lustre that reminded me of picnics in the countryside with Gran and Gramps, where we would set out our food next to a bend in the river and wait for the chub to come out of the shadows. I unfolded myself from the chair and stretched. The sleep had done me good and I felt better, less edgy, more in control.

Gran's car was missing from where she parked it on the road and the house was all quiet. I crossed the patio and peered in through the kitchen window. The clock was placed high, above the pantry door, but I could see it quite clearly. The hands said five past one. I was so cross with myself.

"You're such a lazybones, Jessica," I gasped. "You've wasted a whole Saturday morning and you won't be having any more of those on planet earth."

I'd thought about spending the whole day with Natasha but she'd probably be in town by now. She was obsessed with clothes and I imagined her sweeping through the rails in various stores and putting together some fabulous outfit. I decided the best thing to do was to go straight to her house and wait for her there.

I retraced my steps, back towards the church, past the tennis club and then veered off down a little jitty which was a cut-through between houses. Normally I didn't like using it because the fence was really high on either side, and if anyone was following you it felt really scary, but today there were no such worries because no one could see me.

At the end of the jitty is another road with some big houses and the entrance to the botanical gardens. There's a large patch of grass planted up with daffodils and I stopped to admire them. I'd have liked to have picked some for Nat but I wasn't sure they'd disappear the way the clothes had when I slipped them on, so I just crouched down for a moment and watched a bee dive in, searching for pollen. As soon as I stood up I spotted him. You couldn't mistake that long-legged stride and those broad shoulders. Will was marching towards me, his dog running in front of him, straining at the lead.

"Oh my goodness," I muttered. "It's a good thing he can't see me because, at the moment, that dog probably looks more attractive *and* its coat's all manky from swimming in the brook and rooting about in the woods."

Instinctively I flicked back my hair and licked my lips to give them a bit of gloss. As I watched Will get closer, I mulled over the unfairness of life. The times I had wandered around these streets wearing my best jeans, hair freshly blow-dried, hoping to 'accidentally' bump into him without the hindrance of my brother hanging around. Had it ever happened? Nope. And now here I was, not even thinking that I might see him, and he was making his way towards me. He was frowning, though, and his eyes were fixed towards the pavement. He looked in need of a friendly face. Part of me wished I could just materialise in front of him and say, "Surprise!"

The dog was pulling on the lead, sniffing at the ground and leading him straight towards the grass. It had been named Mr Darcy by Will's mum, and believe me, even if I'd been a four-legged female I don't think I'd have seen the scruffy mutt as a romantic hero, but I loved Will so I pretended to be entranced by the dog. Animals aren't easily fooled, though, and Darcy didn't like me. Perhaps he saw me as some sort of a threat.

Now, as I stood amongst the daffodils, Darcy looked up and started to bark. It didn't take a doggy translator to understand *that* wild woofing. I was definitely not invisible to Darcy and, as I shuffled backwards across the grass, his eyes followed me. The dog was eyeing me up as if I was the primest chump chop for his dinner. Will tugged on the lead but Darcy didn't take any notice. He pulled Will straight towards me and that bark seemed to me to be a complete giveaway, telling the world precisely where I was. It was definitely not a 'Hello Jessica, how nice to see you' type of greeting. Instead, he seemed to be barking a message which said, 'Jessica is gingerly tracing her steps backwards, crushing daffodils under her very chewable trainers. A-ha! Now Jessica can't go back any further and I have her trapped. She is trying to melt into the tree trunk behind her but it isn't working.'

Darcy bared his teeth. He looked as if he was grinning and there was definitely an evil glint in his eye.

"Okay, okay," Will sighed. "What can you smell?"

Tramp, probably, I thought, and guinea pig. I tried to outstare the dog. That's what they said you should do with lions and tigers in the jungle. Obviously it wasn't so hot with mongrels in suburbia. Darcy was right in front of me now. He stuck his nose in my groin. I winced and bit my lip. Again Will tugged on the lead.

"Come on, Darce. Let's wrap it up now."

Darcy growled. Will jerked on the lead and my tormentor allowed himself to be pulled back slightly. I relaxed a little and made a big mistake.

I stuck my tongue out at him. The dog tensed and moved forwards again. I should have seen it coming, moved out of the way. As it was, I just stood there while Darcy cocked his leg and widdled all down my trousers and over my foot. There was enough to fill a bucket. He must have been saving it up all day.

"Good boy," Will said as Darcy scratched at the grass, turfing it all over me.

"Good boy?" I wanted to shriek. "Look at what he's done to me!"

I restrained myself and it was more difficult than trying to stay cool in a sauna.

"Woof!" Darcy said, sounding extremely pleased with himself.

"Come on, boy. Let's go home," Will said.

"You wait," I whispered to the dog. "I'll get my own back when I'm better."

Darcy tossed his head and pranced away, tail wagging, nose in the air.

As I watched Will leave I suddenly remembered that I wasn't going to get better.

Darcy would have the last laugh after all.

NATASHA

The hill leading up to Natasha's house is really steep and I wasn't sure I could make it. As I draped myself over a whitewashed gatepost further down the road, her front door opened.

"Won't be long," Nat called back into the house.

She had teamed what looked like brand new purple joggers with a lilac hoodie and she set off for a run at a gentle pace. I straightened up, sighed and set off after her. Even from the back I could tell that she was thinner. She's always been into sport and exercise and healthy eating, but before the accident she seemed to be taking everything to extremes. It wasn't just the fact that she was getting even more picky with her food. We all felt as if we were treading on eggshells in case she took a casual remark the wrong way. Her mood could change with an exchange of breath. Talking of breath, even though

I was in some sort of strange, suspended state I felt a burning in my chest as I struggled to catch up with her.

"Hang on, Nat," I gasped. "Wait for me."

It was almost as if she heard me and she paused, bending down to re-tie her shoelace. I stopped by her side and bent double for a second. She made me feel such a scruff. Her dark brown hair was tied up in a high ponytail and her eyelids twinkled with frosted mauve shadow. She's always been a perfectionist, but all that effort just to go for a run? It was awesome! Me, I was going for the alternative look. My coral jeans were soaked with dog wee and my hair was adorned with brown leafy bits from Gran's greenhouse.

Mind you, Nat wouldn't have said anything unkind. She'd have wrinkled up her neat, little nose, picked the bits out of my hair and lent me something to wear. Not that I'd have been able to squeeze myself into her size six jeans, even after a month on a drip. I used to be quite envious of her figure. She could wear almost anything and look fantastic, not that she thought so. She was always going on about how fat she was and pinching minuscule amounts of flesh from her hollow thighs. We all told her not to be silly, that she looked great, but I could tell she didn't really believe us.

I'd started to feel a bit helpless. One day, just before the accident, when the two of us were on our own, I did dare to broach the subject.

"You don't want to lose any more weight, Nat," I'd said.

"I don't know what you mean," she replied, pulling at the sleeves of her baggy school jumper.

"I just think you're getting a bit too skinny."

I bit my lip, hoping she wouldn't jump down my throat.

"It can affect your bones, you know. My gran's got small bones and she's always worrying about osteoporosis."

"That's for old people," she shot back.

"Well, what about your periods?"

Her blue eyes flashed back at me. They could look so cold sometimes.

"What about them?"

"They can stop, can't they, if you lose too much weight?"

"I'm fine, Jess, really," she said. "Look, I've got loads to eat here."

I stared into her Tupperware container. She brings salad to school every day – carrot, lettuce, cucumber, tomato, watercress, all chopped up quite small. On Friday, as a special treat, she garnishes it with some meagre flakes of tuna in brine. Yuk! Brine rhymes with whine and I think that's what it makes you want to do. Even in the middle of winter she eats that concoction.

I try to eat my five portions of fruit and veg a day but there's nothing like a piping hot pudding to cheer you up when the weather's horrible. Nat could definitely have done with a bowlful of blackberry and apple crumble. She was always cold, muffling herself up even in summer, but if you tried to push her into eating comfort food she got really snappy. We didn't really mind, though. That was the great thing about our group. You didn't have to always be 'on form' in the same way you did with some other people. No one would dump you for having the occasional grumpy day. Good thing, too, or lately Nat might have had to find herself a new group of friends.

"It doesn't look very filling," I'd persisted as she

picked up three watercress leaves and placed them on her tongue.

"It'll keep me going until supper," she said. "I eat masses then."

I'd gazed at her, wondering if she was speaking the truth, but couldn't make up my mind. It felt so disloyal to think she was lying to me, to her best friends. She wouldn't, would she?

"I've always had a fast metabolism," she added. "My hormones must have sped it up even more. Don't worry, Jess."

But I did worry. We all did, but we didn't know what to do, or how to help.

Nat was picking up speed again but my legs felt as wobbly as a newborn foal's. I concentrated hard, trying to find a rhythm that would enable me to keep up with her.

Is this what it's like being a ghost? I wondered. I'd never really thought about it before but if I had, I knew that I'd have imagined it to be easy, all that wafting about, materialising and disappearing. Now I wondered if they got worn out trying to keep up with the human race. Was it more difficult to make a good job of haunting these days with everyone being so preoccupied and busy, busy, busy? Was it harder for ghosts to make themselves heard because people just didn't have the time to listen properly?

As I floundered away next to Nat, I'd have liked to listen to her and to chat back, not that I'd have been able to say much at that pace. I'd have been happy for her to do most of the talking, to tell me what she'd been up to for the past month, and I would have paid more careful attention than I had ever done before. Instead, Nat popped her earphones in and stared straight ahead. She was totally focused and didn't seem to notice anything around her – the traffic, the trees, the houses, anything. It was as if she was in a totally different place, and it felt a bit lonely to be struggling along beside her knowing that she didn't have a clue that I was there.

I was just about to expire with the effort of it all when Nat stopped and sat down on a low brick wall to check her pedometer. I sank down and let my head drop towards my knees for a moment. Urgh! The unmistakeable aroma of dog's urine wafted under my nostrils. Nat could obviously smell something offensive too, and she pulled a face while checking the distance she'd run, how many steps taken, calories burned, that sort of thing. Her fingers looked in danger of snapping as they punched at the buttons.

I'd never noticed the blueness of her veins before or how the skin was slack and translucent around her knuckles, but my observation skills were improving no end. When you can't speak to anyone there's no point thinking about what to say next, so you notice your surroundings more. You pick up on signals that you might otherwise miss, and Nat's hands were giving off serious warning signals. I had to help. But what could I do?

You cannot die, Jessica. You have to live.

I tried my very best to push the thought away. I told myself that it was stupid, impossible, that I was living in fairytale land. But the thought had attached itself to me like a leech and it wasn't going anywhere without a fight.

Nat was barely out of breath when we got back to the house but her cheeks were a pretty pink and her eyes sparkled. The kitchen window opened.

 135

"Tea will be ready soon, Natasha," her mum called. "Can you come and set the table?"

Something swirled around in my stomach. Hunger.

"Now that," I said, looking up at the sky, half expecting to see Darren sitting on a fluffy white cloud, "is really cruel."

Nat's mum writes cookery books. She's always trying out new recipes and the house can be scented with all sorts of delicious things that caress your nostrils: cinnamon, orange, rosemary, onions slowly caramelised in olive oil, and vanilla were my favourites. My mum's cooking was fine but she wasn't very adventurous, and since Dad's affair she seemed to have lost interest altogether. I loitered by the fridge as Nat set three places. She methodically straightened the knives and forks, put out side plates with napkins folded neatly on top, and lit two candles. It looked so pretty when she'd finished.

Next time I set the table at home, I'll make more of an effort, I thought.

Then it hit me again, like a tidal wave crashing

against rocks. There wasn't going to be a next time.

"Is there a funny smell in here?" Nat's mum lifted her face from what she was stirring.

"I thought it was supper," Nat responded.

I frowned at her. There was no need for that.

"Are you sure you haven't trodden in something while you were out?" Her mum was a picture of calm but I could see the hurt in her eyes. Nat turned up the soles of her trainers and shook her head.

"Well, take them off anyway," her mum said, "and perhaps you'd better go and change out of those clothes before we eat. You don't want to spill anything down that top. It's such a pretty colour. While you're upstairs you can tell Dean that supper will be ready in two minutes."

I followed Nat up the stairs and into her room. I loved that room. The walls are washed with a light shade of lilac – it *is* her favourite colour – and on the bed are a selection of artistically arranged cushions in various hues of pink. On the bedside table is a big photo of her dad. It was taken on holiday in Spain, the year before he was killed in a motorway pile-up. Nat was only five but said she could remember lots about him. She felt that she had to keep his memory alive for Dean because he'd only been a toddler when it happened and her mum didn't talk about their dad very much. He'd gone to work one day as usual and not come back.

Nat hadn't gone to the funeral and she felt cheated. Although we all said that her mum had only done what she thought was best at the time, a small part of me felt sad that Nat hadn't had the chance to say goodbye. She talked to that photo of her dad. I was the only one who knew that. I don't think she meant to tell me but it just slipped out one day. Immediately her eyes widened and her mouth fell open in alarm. It was as if she'd thought that I might laugh. I'd never do that, not in a million years. I thought it was cool she talked to her dad's photo.

"You won't tell anyone, Jess, will you?" she'd said. "I don't want anyone else to know. They might think it's a bit weird."

I was a bit taken aback.

"No they won't."

She'd shrugged.

"All the same, I'd rather you didn't. I'd rather it was our secret."

She'd held out her hand and I'd hesitated for a moment. Not because I'm a blabbermouth – that wasn't the reason. I'm actually quite good at keeping things to myself. After Gramps died I looked up at the sky sometimes and sent silent messages to him or asked for advice. That was *my* secret. I hadn't even told Sara.

At that moment, though, I'd been on the point of telling Nat and even confiding that I was sure Gramps sent me answers to my questions, but something stopped me. I'd stared at Nat's palm and knew that I should feel flattered that she'd told me something so personal, but part of me wished that she hadn't. I wanted to be a good friend to everyone in the group, not just to Nat, and that meant sharing things. It's one thing keeping your own secrets; it's quite another keeping someone else's. Gran says that life is full of compromise and maybe she's right, but it didn't make holding out on my friends any easier. All the same, I took hold of Nat's hand and promised to zip my lips.

Now I squeezed myself into a corner of her bedroom. I might have been invisible but in enclosed spaces I still felt the need to keep myself hidden as much as possible. The wooden floorboards felt hard against my bum and my legs were definitely aching from that run. I shifted to get more comfortable and turned my attention back to Nat. How on earth would she cope with my death? One day I had been at school, pairing up with her in chemistry, virtually setting fire to her hair with a Bunsen burner, and the next day I was in hospital, never to return to our life together. It wasn't the same as what happened to her dad, but it was similar and I felt beside myself with worry.

Nat took off the joggers and top. She was too busy inspecting herself in the full-length mirror to hear me gasp. Her shoulder blades jutted out like chicken wings as she grabbed a sliver of flesh from her thigh and grimaced, pressing tightly, as if she wanted to bruise herself. I wanted to leap up and stop her, to wrap my arms around her and hug her as tightly as we both could bear, but she looked as brittle as a brandy snap. Standing in her pretty blue and white striped underwear she didn't look strong enough to support her own weight, let alone do normal, everyday things like walk to school, lift a rucksack or have a hug.

The signs had been there all along, of course; the way she was always first or last in the changing rooms when we got changed for PE, the way her tracky bottoms were always slipped on under her skirt, the way she said she'd got her period if we suggested going swimming in the holidays and the way she never liked to share a changing room when we went shopping.

I couldn't hide from the facts any longer, couldn't file them away in that place where unpleasant things are stored, known but not acknowledged. As she stood there I could count every single rib, and her hip bones looked like wire coat-hangers forcing their way out through her skin. Those pipe-cleaner men we made in Year One had more substantial frames.

How could you do this, Nat? I raged inside. How could you deliberately put your life at risk when I have no choice about mine?

"Natasha!"

Her mum's voice swivelled up the stairs.

"Come on! It's going cold."

Nat slipped on a baggy top and stepped into some jeans, which looked as if they were two sizes too big, and left the room.

The dog wee was permeating my nasal passages more forcefully now, a permanent reminder of Will but not the sort I'd dreamed of. Nat's dressing table was overflowing with perfume bottles. I snatched one called Peachy Paradise and sprayed myself liberally. My image in the mirror appeared stronger. I could make out my eyebrows, which needed plucking, and the mole on my wrist. I was confused. If I could see myself more clearly, did that mean I was becoming more visible to other people as well?

I tiptoed downstairs and sidled into the kitchen, half expecting someone to look up and say, "Hey Jess, what are you doing there?"

In their different ways everyone was too intent on the food to pick up on my presence.

"I can't eat that much," Nat groaned, staring at the plate of fish pie in front of her.

"Of course you can," her mum said briskly. "You

need to keep your strength up. You've been looking tired recently."

Tired? I thought. Was that some sort of code word? Couldn't she see that her daughter was wasting away?

Nat filled a tumbler of water to the brim and sat down. My nostrils twitched like a rabbit's. Alongside the dog wee and Peachy Paradise I could definitely detect the smell of fish and cheese sauce. It was a couple of minutes before I picked up on the painful tension battling with the scented steam which swirled up from the three white plates.

Nat prodded a prawn with her fork, tentatively, as a naturalist might awaken a poisonous insect. Her terror was barely concealed. I could read her mind, see her adding up the enemy calories. She pushed the prawn to one side and selected a button mushroom. Slowly, the fork moved to her mouth. She pulled a face. One mushroom was chewed over and over. Water. A huge gulp to force it down. No one watching her, yet everyone acutely aware; the whole room holding its breath.

"You know I don't like fish in sauce," she whined.

"It's good for you." Her mum tried to keep it light. "Full of calcium."

"It's disgusting."

"I'll have yours," Dean said, making a grab for the plate.

Quick as a flash, Nat's mum slapped his hand away.

"No need for that. There's plenty more in the oven."

Come on, Nat, I willed. Eat up. I remembered primary school, when we couldn't leave the table until our plates were clean. She's always been a picky eater, and one day Nat sat there for two hours refusing to eat her cheese flan. I could have told the teacher there and then not to bother. Even at six years old she was stubborn, and I knew she wouldn't give in. I foresaw a repeat performance as Nat's mum sat like a guard at the top of the table.

"What's that smell?" Dean asked. "Is it you, Nat? I think that perfume has gone off."

She stood up, flinging back her chair and sending it skittling across the floor.

"It's not me," she shrieked. "It's probably this fish. It must be off."

"Natasha, don't." Her mum looked tearful now,

wounded. "Sit down and eat something, please."

"I'm not hungry," Natasha shouted. "Why don't you all just leave me alone?"

I flattened myself against the fridge as she stormed past me towards the stairs.

Silence. Nat's mum put her head in her hands. Dean stared out of the window. Helplessness clogged the room. Then Dean reached over, took Natasha's plate and started to eat what she had left.

I stood for a moment, as if in the wake of a storm, waiting for everything to settle, waiting for my confused thoughts to form themselves into orderly sentences.

I'd always felt a bit protective of Nat. We all had. We didn't talk about her behind her back – not much, anyway. But everyone – Sara, Kelly, Yasmin and me – worried about how emotionally fragile she was – 'highly strung', Gran would probably have called it. We'd tried to support her as best we could and we'd thought we were doing a good job, but now, looking back, I wondered if there was a cut-off point – a point beyond which none of us were prepared to go because of the consequences.

Deep down I think I'd known that she'd got an eating problem but I'd been afraid to confront her in case she cut me off, in case she decided that she didn't want to be my friend any more.

"All the same, Jess," I muttered to myself, as I watched her mum clear away the plates, "you should have done something – talked to her mum, the teachers, anything instead of pretending it wasn't happening."

And then what? Would Yasmin, Kelly and Sara have supported me? Would Nat have hated me? Would she have blamed the others too and finished her friendship with all of us? If I'd made too many waves it would have changed things between us all, and at the time I couldn't face up to that.

I went back upstairs to join her. She was sprawled against the pink cushions texting and listening to her iPod. I sat on the chair by her dressing table and draped my arms over its wooden back so that I could look at her. The monochrome light just accentuated her unhappiness and the air in the room was thick with denial. She used to be so pretty but now her hair had lost its gloss and her skin had a sallow tinge. Her loveliness seemed to have shrunk along with her body. Even her character seemed changed. That cruel streak that I had witnessed in the kitchen wasn't the real Nat, but I was sure that she was still there somewhere, hibernating beneath the gauntness. She put down her phone and closed her eyes.

Oh, Nat! I thought. I wish I could talk to you, get you to see sense. You don't want to end up in hospital like me, with a tube down your throat and Darren the Angel of Death licking his lips in the shadows.

She looked so frail. Instinctively, I knew that the shock of hearing my disembodied voice was the last thing she needed – but I was desperate to do something – anything. I didn't think she was asleep but if she did drift off...

Could I make a difference after all? After Gramps died, Gran started having panic attacks and she bought a relaxation CD which she played to herself every night. She said that even when you're asleep your brain is receptive to sounds and ideas. I tried it when revising for my history exam. I'd recorded a load of facts on this little Dictaphone that Dad uses for work and played it back just as I was drifting off to sleep. It seemed to help. I could barely believe it when my paper came back with 78 per cent and an exclamation mark scrawled at the top. If it had worked for Gran and me, could it work for Nat too?

I watched and waited, enduring the tick of the clock on the wall behind me. 'Tick tock, death knocks,' it seemed to say.

"Maybe for me, but not for Nat," I whispered back. "At least not if I can help it."

Her breathing became more even and I watched as her eyelids settled into stillness.

Eventually I crawled across the floor, getting closer and closer to the bed. I was so scared that she would wake up, that I would do more harm than good. I'd been shocked into bravery with the tramp, but it's different when you've got time to think, when it's someone you know, someone you love. There was this hammering in my heart space which seemed to go boom boom and fill the room, but she didn't stir. I knelt back on my heels next to the bed and stared at the photo of her dad. Tucked into a corner of the frame was a picture of me, laughing as I messed about in the hammock in Sara's garden last year.

"Come on, Jess. Be brave," I murmured.

I teased out one earplug. She stirred slightly and I froze, but she didn't open her eyes, so I put my mouth very close to her and whispered so softly that I could barely hear myself.

"Natty, it's me, Jess."

I paused, waiting for her to jump up and hit her head on the sloping ceiling before flying out of the room in a total panic. But it was okay. She was still asleep.

"I've really missed you, Nat, and I'm worried. You've got to start eating or you'll end up in hospital – or worse. Listen to me, Nat, please. You're not well. It's time to face up to it. You mustn't be scared. Everyone wants to help you. I'll be with you, holding your hand. You won't know I'm there, but I will be. I'll try and do a deal with Darren so that I can come back and help. I promise."

I imagined those words threading their way

into her brain like a subliminal message, registering, marinating, healing. I didn't know if I'd be able to keep my promise, but sometimes you have to say things you're not sure of. Sometimes, that's the only way forward. My head almost touched hers. I felt hot and clammy, but she stayed still. Only her gold hoop earring moved as I breathed out my message.

"Nat, if you can't do this for me, do it for your dad. We don't want you joining us just yet. You've got a wonderful life in front of you."

Was it working, or were those words going in one ear and straight out the other?

"Believe, Jess," I murmured to myself. "Believe that you can make a difference."

She sighed and turned her head away. I leaned forwards, my lips almost brushing her ear lobe.

"Please, please listen to me, Natty," I whispered, a large lump forming in my throat. "Thinner thighs really aren't worth dying for. Believe me. I know."

All of a sudden her eyes flicked open. I jumped back and scrabbled to my feet.

"Jess?"

My throat went into a spasm. I backed towards

the door as she turned on the bedside lamp, sat up and looked around.

"Jess?"

Could she see me, after all? I stopped, almost spoke, and then I realised that she was looking at my photograph, not at me. Disappointment flooded through me and Nat shivered, rubbing the tops of her arms. She swung her legs over the edge of the bed, a crease appearing between her eyebrows. She held my photograph between her fingers and moved over to the mirror, turning herself slowly, viewing her body from every angle.

"I thought you were here, Jess," she said, "in the room, with me, talking to me."

I was. I am. I so wanted to say those words but I clamped my hand over my lips.

Nat gathered up a handful of loose denim and pulled her jeans tight.

"Thinner thighs aren't worth dying for," she murmured.

She *had* heard me. I couldn't believe it. I was about to punch the air in triumph when she turned towards the door and rushed past so fast that

I was almost knocked to the ground.

"Mum! Mum!" she shouted, stumbling down the stairs.

"What?" her mother called back. "What's the matter?"

"It's Jess," she gasped. "You've got to ring the hospital to check on her. I need to know that she's okay. I need to know that nothing's happened."

"I'm sure we'd have heard..." her mum began, but I heard Nat yank the phone out of its holder.

"Please, Mum," she begged. "Just do it."

I stood on the landing to listen and watch as they made the call.

"There's no change, sweetheart," her mum said, bending to wrap her arms around her daughter as Nat sank onto the hard floor and started to sob. Even Dean emerged from his room and went downstairs to place a comforting hand on Nat's shoulder.

"I thought I heard her," she sobbed. "It was as if she was there, right next to me."

She looked up at her mother wide-eyed.

"I thought she was a ghost. I thought she must be..."

"It was a dream," her mother said. "That's all. Let's get a cup of tea."

I sat at the top of the stairs as they closed the kitchen door behind them.

"That's all you're going to be in the future, Jess," I said to myself. "When people think about you, it'll be like a dream. Even with photographs and videos and keepsakes, eventually it will feel as if you didn't really exist at all."

SUPPORT

SATURDAY, 4 MARCH – 8.37 P.M.

Where did I belong? Not here in the real world any more, not at Nat's house or Sara's or even my own. My spiritual energy plummeted like an out-of-control lift. Down, down, down it went. It was like hitting that car all over again as my emotions slammed into me.

"Bye, Nat," I said through the solid kitchen door. "Take care of yourself."

I let myself out of the house and slumped onto the pretty white bench in her front garden. It had always seemed a strange place for anyone to want to sit when the back garden was so long and private, but I was grateful for it now. The darkness enveloped me but I was too drained to be scared of it any more. Light spilled from the surrounding houses. Everyone was carrying on without me. I sat, stranded in my loneliness.

"Come along, Jessica. Let's have you back in the world of the living."

Mrs Baxter's voice wrenched me from my stupor. Was there no getting away from this woman? Would she follow me to the afterlife with equations and impossible problems? If three hundred and sixty-five angels have seventeen harps between them, on how many days would each angel be able to play?

I smiled slightly. Actually, back in the land of the living she'd been quite nice to me, despite my uselessness. Now I realised that what I had seen as nagging was really her weird teacherly way of encouraging me.

"Sorry for being such a pain, Mrs B," I whispered into the night. "I bet your life's much easier without me. I bet Set Three are racing ahead now, without me to hold them back."

"Will you stop putting yourself down all the time, Jessica!" she replied. Her voice was clipped, but not in a sharp way, and I could picture her eyes, astute but kind. She just wanted the best for me. "Let's have some positive thinking here."

"Okay," I muttered. "I'll whack the self pity on the head."

She nodded and her face floated away, as if her job was done for now.

My legs had stiffened. I rested my hands on my knees and wiggled my toes. I could feel them tip-tapping against the rubber tips of the trainers. What did it all mean? I wasn't quite sure, but my body was trying to talk to me, in its own way, and one thing I did know was that trekking all the way back to Gran's wasn't a viable option. I shivered and wished that I'd borrowed one of Nat's coats. A hat, scarf and gloves would have been good too. In human terms I was a chilly-boned sort of person and always hogged the fire at home, but in my present state, surely cold was not good? Surely cold meant the end was getting closer?

Fear fluttered in my chest like a trapped insect. In spite of my legs' protests I knew, deep in my cobwebbed brain, that I had to keep moving. I wasn't sure if I could succumb to hypothermia or pick up other human ailments, but I wasn't prepared to risk it. No way was I going to let the Grim Reaper claim me yet. As if to reward my determination, a lorry sporting large green lettering rumbled past the end of the road. I offered up a prayer of thanks to the god of supermarkets and began to walk.

The harsh lights of the superstore made me recoil, but at the same time I'd never been so grateful to trudge through those sliding doors, and this time I activated them all on my own. I dodged the people who were milling around the flowers at the entrance, crossing my fingers that the lilies wouldn't make me sneeze, and headed off towards the clothes section. It was quiet by comparison. There was quite a selection to choose from as the new summer stock was beginning to fill the rails. I wasn't sure whether my sense of smell was returning to normal or whether urine became more pungent at night, but I definitely stank to high heaven! I had to get out of those jeans. The beloved trainers would have to go too.

I chose some charcoal-coloured leggings and a pair of irresistible lemon-yellow ballet pumps with a white trim and tiny little bows on the front. They were quite angelic-looking, which seemed to suit the sudden aspirational thought that had

157

popped into my head. My destiny as a high flyer on earth might have been dashed, but who was to say that I wouldn't find my true calling in eternity? "Angel Jessica at the ready," I murmured, untying the trainers and kicking them beneath a rail of trousers.

I couldn't just pick up the leggings and take them to the changing room. Someone would be bound to notice them floating spookily through the air. I sighed.

"Okay Jess," I said to myself. "You're going to have to change here, in public, in full view of anyone who turns down that aisle. You're going to have to stand in the middle of the store in your knickers.

"Get a grip," I added. "It's not as if everyone can see you. You're invisible, remember."

"But what if I'm not?" the opposing side of my brain asked. "What if I suddenly materialise, or what if there's someone here with extra sensory powers who makes a fuss and everyone comes running?"

I had visions of being encircled by a crowd of shoppers, all gawping at me.

"Just get on with it, Jessica," Mrs Baxter used to say. "The longer you wait, the harder it will seem."

"Okay, okay," I murmured. "I've got to do this.

I can't walk around in these stinky trousers any longer. Even I am starting to feel slightly sick of the smell."

I waited for a lull in customers and dropped my jeans to the floor. A middle-aged lady pushed her trolley around the corner and I cursed silently.

"Go away," I mouthed as I pressed myself back against a rail of T-shirts and edged the coral jeans behind me, out of sight. I seemed to stand there for ages while she made up her mind between a white shirt with a black trim or a black shirt with a white trim.

Eventually she moved on and I was able to wriggle into the leggings. It occurred to me that, officially, I was stealing, but I hoped that God would forgive me. After all, the circumstances were fairly exceptional.

The lights and the effort of changing clothes had warmed me. I almost fancied I could feel blood coursing through my non-existent veins. The supermarket didn't close until ten o'clock so I mooched around among the shoppers, looking at all the things I'd never get the chance to eat again:

potato smileys, coffee ice cream, salt and vinegar crisps, watermelon. I stood next to the bakery section for ages just breathing in the beautiful yeasty smell, and even dared myself to go behind the counter so that I could get a better look at the glistening chocolate éclairs and lemon iced buns. Suddenly I felt so sad, and something wet dropped onto the meringues that the assistant was placing in a box next to me. She looked up at the ceiling to see if the roof was leaking and so did I.

"That's odd," she muttered.

I stepped back. There was a strange sensation on my face, a salty taste trickling over my lips. I wiped my hand across my cheek. It came away coated in dampness. There was no mistake – I was crying, and my tears were dropping onto that meringue.

I needed a distraction from my sadness so I decided to get in some practice for the Saturday job that I would now never have. As the shoppers began to thin out, I surreptitiously began to reorganise the yoghurt section, making sure that the ones with the nearest sell-by date were at the front. To start with it was surprisingly absorbing but then I began to think about my own sell-by date, so I decided to move on. For some totally illogical reason I ended up at the fresh fish counter where the deal of the day, half a dozen whole mackerel, lay shiny and lifeless on a bed of crushed ice.

"That'll be you soon," sang a little voice inside my head.

I dropped my head into my hands. I might as well just give up now and send a message to Darren to beam me up. All of this invisibility was so stressful, and it was just delaying the inevitable, wasn't it?

"You're just overtired, pet."

I started and looked around. I knew that voice.

Gramps was standing beside me, right next to the salmon. He hated fish, couldn't even bear the smell of it cooking, so I knew I wasn't imagining it. This was the last place on earth I would have expected him to materialise. He was wearing his favourite olive-green cardigan with the leather buttons and I could feel his phantom breath on my face. It smelled fresh and minty like it used to. He always had a packet of extra-strong mints in his pocket.

"Gramps," I whispered. "Is it really you?"

He smiled and nodded, a fraction of a frown crossing his forehead.

"Of course it is, petal. You haven't forgotten me already, have you?"

"No, no."

He beckoned me over to a quiet corner by the soft drinks.

"I just never thought I would see you here."

I paused and rolled my eyes towards the ceiling.

"Up there, yes, but not down here."

"You sounded as if you needed a bit of company," he said.

I bit my lip. I could feel my teeth digging in. How was that possible? I just didn't know.

I didn't know anything any more, what was real and what wasn't. Was Gramps just a figment of my imagination? Was I going mad?

"Jess!" He was still there, still talking to me. "What you need is a good night's sleep. Everything will seem better in the morning."

"You think?" I asked, shaking my head. "I'm not

so sure."

He didn't touch me, and I daren't reach out in case he disappeared before I was ready.

"Don't give up, my Jess. You're not a quitter. You've still got people to see and things to do." He looked serious all of a sudden. "These visits could be more important than you realise, for them as well as you."

"What do you mean?"

He looked around and put his finger to his lips.

"I mustn't say or I'll get us both into trouble."

"Gramps, tell me, please. I don't understand."

"You will, sweetheart," he said. "Just keep going, keep fighting, and you will."

I frowned, blinked and brushed my eyes with my sleeve. I must have blinked Gramps away because suddenly he'd gone.

"No!" I wanted to shout. "Come back!"

Instead, I crossed my arms over my body and hugged myself, but it wasn't enough. I wanted someone else to hug me – Mum, Gran, even Dad. It was their solid, warm, strong arms I needed to feel wrapped around me, not my own.

Gramps was right. I needed to sleep. I wandered back to the clothes section and investigated the changing rooms. The one at the far end was the biggest and by now it was nearly closing time so it was empty. I pulled the curtain across and sat on the plastic stool, waiting for the lights to dim and the shelf-stackers to go home. Eventually I had the whole place to myself so I ventured out of my hidey hole and grabbed two duvets and a pillow from 'Homewares'.

It's funny how when you've got set bed-times or school the next morning all you want to do is push the boundaries, to stay up late watching DVDs or chatting on Facebook. If I'd wanted to I could have stayed up all night in that supermarket. I could have tried on every item of clothing in the store, picked out a good book or flicked through all the magazines. I did want to stay awake – sleeping seemed like such a waste of the time I had left – but I felt weighed down by tiredness. I made myself a little nest with one duvet, pulled the other one over the top and collapsed into a deep, deep sleep.

The rings jangled on the metal rail as the curtain was

yanked back. My eyelids zipped open and fluttered nervously at a small, serious child, her gaze fixed on my mound of bedding. I was almost completely enveloped. Even if I was real, she'd barely have been able to see me. Only the top half of my face protruded, but the way she stared made me feel uneasy. There was the same look in her eyes as there had been with Will's dog Darcy: an intensity that made me feel very, very nervous.

We eye-balled each other for what seemed like absolutely ages until finally someone called her. She turned, reluctantly, and then she lifted her chubby little hand and shyly wiggled her fingers. It wasn't a proper wave but it was definitely a wave, and I panicked. I leapt up and stood on the stool. I'm not sure why but it seemed the right thing to do in case someone came to search the changing room. I waited and waited but nothing happened, no security guard came running, ready to strong-arm me into a waiting police car.

"Relax, Jess," I told myself, but that's easier said than done when you're a mishmash of nerves. "Look at yourself. You're still invisible. Okay, so you're getting bit brighter, and there's a sort of pastel hue around your edges, but no one will notice you. They're all too busy with their own lives. Talking of which, you need to get on with yours."

The store was starting to get busy and it was already ten forty-five. Time seemed to be speeding up and my life was running out faster than a split bag of sugar. If only I'd realised before the accident how quickly everything could change. Would I have done some things differently? Maybe, but maybe not.

"There's not much point thinking about that now," I said to myself. "It's too late."

Too late – how I hated those two little words. I grabbed a raspberry-coloured quilted jacket and headed for the exit.

Hooray! The sun was shining. It felt wrong to have a surge of happiness when everything was such a disaster. It reminded me of how people had laughed at Gramps's wake and how disapproving I had been. Now I wanted to hold on to my happy feeling. It made me feel light and hopeful and gave me the strange sense that I was in control. And I was – up to a point. I could decide who to see next, Yasmin or Kelly.

It was just a pity that Darren hadn't loaned me a pair of wings to get from A to B – that would have made things a whole lot easier.

While I loitered by the trolley bay, trying to decide, there was a rush of icy cold air and I pulled the jacket tightly around me. There was a funny sensation all along my arms, similar to goose-pimples erupting, and in my heart space a racing, fearful feeling. He was here somewhere, watching me, waiting to appear. I felt sick, and started to move back behind a pillar. Stupid, stupid me. There was no escape from him.

Darren materialised in an instant, blocking my path, his wings outstretched, hand put up in front of me like a stop sign.

"We need to talk," he said.

And it suddenly occurred to me. It was Sunday the fifth of March. It was the day I was originally meant to die.

SECRETS

SUNDAY, 5 MARCH – 11.07 A.M.

I didn't think I had ever felt more scared in my entire life. He must know about my visit to Gran's house, I thought. I had broken the rules again. He had come to fetch me.

"Play it cool, Jess," I said to myself. "Keep calm."

"I-is there something wr-wrong?" I stammered, my teeth chattering even though the sun felt warm on my back.

He sighed and studied me with those X-ray eyes.

"What do you think?"

I shrugged, hoping to fool him.

"According to the *Oxford English Dictionary*," he stated in a rather pained voice, "a rule is a principle, regulation or maxim governing individual conduct. Now, you seem to be an intelligent girl,

Jessica Rowley, so exactly what is it about that definition that you don't understand?"

I looked down at the ground. His feet were bare and very pale. I wondered if he felt the cold. I held up my hands in surrender.

"Okay, I admit it. I went to Gran's house but I didn't go inside. I slept in the greenhouse and I didn't see her."

The desperation in my voice bounced off the concrete pillar.

"But you have seen someone else, haven't you?"

"No, I haven't. I promise. Oh, you mean Will? That was an accident. I bumped into him while I was on my way to Nat's. You can't blame me for that. I've lived around here for my whole life. I'm going to see people I know from time to time."

He raised both eyebrows.

"Actually, I didn't know about him," he said, and I inwardly cursed for giving myself away.

"That must have been unfortunate, bumping into the love of your life looking like that."

 169

I ignored the insult.

"I'm talking about someone else. You had a visitor last night, didn't you?"

He obviously meant Gramps. I pressed my lips together, took my time in answering. I'd learned my lesson. I wasn't going to admit to anything unless I absolutely had to.

"Did I?"

Darren put his hands on his hips and tilted his head to one side. The sunlight caught the edge of his halo and dazzled my eyes.

"Jessica, I'm not stupid, and you are a very bad liar."

"Actually, if you're going to be picky, that wasn't quite a lie."

I blinked up at him. He didn't look quite so tall. Was I growing? How odd was that? Surely you started to shrink in your last days.

"Oh dear, dear, dear," he gasped. "Now you're answering back. This isn't good at all. I *know* that your grandfather has been to see you and I hope he hasn't been putting any silly ideas into your head. Some of the dearly departed can become a bit rebellious and take it upon themselves to meddle where they shouldn't."

That sounded like Gramps. He was never one for lots of rules and restrictions.

"He won't get into trouble, will he?"

"Not if you tell me what he said."

So Darren the Angel of Death was not invincible. He didn't know everything. He wasn't everywhere. Maybe I could have some secrets after all. I lowered my eyelids, dropped my shoulders and tried to look defeated.

"I was upset, that's all. Gramps came to comfort me. It was nice. He made me feel better."

Oops! Wrong word. I knew as soon as I'd said it.

"Better! You're not meant to feel better."

If his wings hadn't been spread out wide I reckon he'd have shot straight up through his halo like a rocket.

"No, no, not better in that way," I protested. "I meant better in a sort of accepting way, better about what is going to happen to me."

He looked relieved, then doubtful.

"And he didn't say anything else?"

I looked up, deciding to outstare him.

"Like what?"

A muscle in his airbrushed face twitched unexpectedly. He grimaced as if he'd swallowed something really unpleasant.

"He didn't try to give you…" He could barely get the word out. "Hope?"

Something sparked inside of me. It was as if a little flame had been lit. Would he notice?

"Of course not."

My voice sounded firm and convincing. All the same, I waited for him to scoff, to accuse me of lying again. He didn't, so I decided to push my luck.

"There wouldn't be any point, would there?"

I watched him carefully, standing my ground. Did I detect a flicker of anxiety in those baby-blue eyes?

"Absolutely not," he retorted, a petulant look on his face. "None at all."

I don't believe you. The thought snaked through me like a waft of pure oxygen, and that little flame felt as if it was burning brighter, stretching higher.

"You don't have to worry," I said. "I'll be there well before my appointed time on Wednesday unless…"

I clenched and unclenched my fists, stretched out my fingers, tried to release the tension that held me rigid.

"… unless you've come to take me back with you now."

He pressed a hand to his forehead.

"Why is this job so complicated?" he cried. "Why can't you just do as I ask? Then everything would be fine."

He seemed to be getting a bit overwrought.

"I'm sorry. I'll try. I promise."

He seemed to relax a little. So did I.

"There was one question I wanted to ask…"

He rolled his eyes.

"What now?"

"Can I go back to school? Is that allowed? I'd just like to see all of my friends together, hang around with them at break, maybe even sit in on a few lessons."

He flapped his wings and fluffed out his feathers.

"You're a glutton for punishment, aren't you?"

I shrugged. "Lessons don't seem so bad when you know that you're never going to have to sit

173

through another one and be set piles of homework at the end of it."

"I don't suppose it would do any harm," he said.

"Thank you."

He looked surprised, as if he didn't get many thanks.

"One more thing before you go."

"Oh for goodness' sake," he chuntered. "You're turning into a full-time job."

"I want to go to visit my friend Kelly next, and she lives over on the other side of the park. I don't suppose there's any way you could give me a lift, is there, or lend me a few magical feathers so that I can fly? All of this getting around from one place to another is quite hard work and wastes a lot of time. Time is a bit of an issue for me."

"Sorree!" he said. "No can do."

I must have looked really fed up because all of a sudden he decided to take pity on me.

"Oh, come on then," he said, grabbing my hand, "if it will keep you happy."

I grinned.

"It will."

"At last," he said with an exaggerated flutter of his eyelashes and the hint of a smile at the corner of his lips. "At last she's happy. Just don't tell anyone about this when you get to the other side or they'll think I'm going soft."

"Hang on!"

I pulled him back as he started to flap his wings.

"I should have known there'd be something else," he said.

"You won't fly too high, will you? It's just that I don't like heights."

He laughed. It was like a thousand wind chimes tinkling into the distance. Several people pushing their trolleys across the car park turned and looked around.

"You're such a wimp, Jessica Rowley," he said, still chuckling. "To think that I was worried about you reneging on our deal."

I blinked.

"Were you?"

Surprise fizzed inside of me as if I'd eaten one of those hot French radishes which Dad likes to grow.

"Why?"

He did a funny little twist of his lips.

"I thought I detected a stubborn streak," he said. "That spells trouble. The stubborn ones can put up a bit of resistance." He paused and smiled. For an angel of death, it was a surprisingly warm and genuine smile. "But you're too much of a scaredy-cat for that."

He held up his hand and gave me a high five.

"You're all right, Jessica Rowley."

"Thanks!"

He checked his watch.

"Can we go now?" he asked. "I have got other people to deal with, you know."

I nodded, clung on tight between his wings, and closed my eyes as we twirled up into the air.

He didn't fly too high and eventually I plucked up the courage to open first one eye and then the other. We skimmed the rooftops, sometimes seeming to miss the ridges and chimneys by centimetres. The air rushed past me, making my eyes water and my nose run. I couldn't speak, and every now and then I stretched out my arm and pointed in the right direction. He landed just outside Kelly's front door.

"See ya soon!" he said, as I slid from his back.

"Not too soon," I murmured, sending him a small wave as he soared up towards the clouds, where he belonged.

Kelly

SUNDAY, 5 MARCH – 11.57 A.M.

There was a lot of shouting and yelling coming from Kelly's back garden. Her little brothers, Luke and Simon, were obviously playing football. I padded down the side passage and gently lifted the latch on the blue wooden gate. There was washing blowing on the line and the sliding patio door that led from the kitchen was half open. I could see Kelly standing at the sink as I stepped up into the house. Her head was bent as she concentrated on peeling potatoes and there was a delicious smell of roast meat coming from the oven. She was wearing pale denim jeans with a lemon T-shirt and her blonde, curly hair was tied back with a royal blue ribbon. As I stood watching her, a football hurtled in from the garden, skidded across the kitchen floor and slammed into the back of her legs.

178

"Goal!" Luke shouted, jumping up and down before running around the garden with his arms outstretched, as if he was an aeroplane.

"Watch out!" Kelly called, marching over to the window. "If you can't play sensibly you'll have to come inside."

She sounded really severe, not that Luke seemed to take much notice as he ran into the kitchen and snatched the ball back. He took up position exactly where he had been before and prepared to shoot again.

Kelly shook her head and closed the patio door before walking back to the sink and plopping the last potato into a saucepan of cold water. There was a mug of coffee on the work surface and she picked it up, raising it to her lips. With her other hand she fingered the pendant hanging around her neck. It was a turquoise enamelled butterfly which I had bought for her last birthday. Even though Kelly is mad about sport, she's still delicate and graceful. As soon as I'd spotted it, the butterfly had reminded me of her. It had seemed like the perfect present but, until now, I'd never seen her wear it. I'd begun to wonder if it wasn't really her taste after all.

Kelly's quite a private person and doesn't open up very easily, but once you get to know her properly, once she learns to trust you, you've got a friend for life. I hadn't been to her house much – none of us had. It's quite small, and before her mum left there were six of them living there: Kelly, her parents, her two younger brothers and her little sister Georgia. Now there were just four. When Kelly's mum walked out she took Georgia with her. That was nearly two years ago, when Kelly was twelve and Georgia only three. There was no warning. One Wednesday afternoon Kelly got home from school and found a note on the kitchen table. Her mum had upped and gone to Scotland with a man from over the road. Until that teatime, Kelly and her dad hadn't a clue that anything was wrong.

After the shock of the first couple of weeks she didn't really talk about it much, but I knew that her dad had gone to court to try to get access to Georgia. The trouble was, her mum made it really difficult. A couple of times Kelly, her dad and the boys all trooped up to Scotland to see Georgia. It was a complete waste of time and money because on both occasions Kelly's mum had taken Georgia away on holiday, supposedly at the last moment. Right! If you believe that you'll believe anything. None of them had seen Georgia since the day she left.

I wondered if Kelly's mum had any idea what she'd done to them all. I wondered if she even cared. Kelly's dad got depressed and he couldn't work for a while. For a few months before my accident Kelly wouldn't come out with us as much because her dad found the boys a bit much to cope with if she wasn't around. It all seemed so unfair to me.

As I stood in the kitchen I could just see her dad, sitting in the living room watching television with the sound turned down.

"Dad," Kelly called, "do you want broccoli or carrots with the roast lamb?"

"Don't mind."

The voice which filtered back to the kitchen was totally flat.

I saw Kelly's shoulders drop.

"Okay," she said in a bright but false tone. "We'll have broccoli then. The boys like that better."

There was silence from the other room. She lifted a pile of dirty washing from the floor and stuffed it into the machine. I padded across to the doorway to get a better look at her father. He was slumped in a chair, and on the table next to him was a glass of water and several containers of pills. I willed him to get up and help her but he just sat there, eyes fixed on the TV screen.

I moved back into the kitchen and sat on the worn navy-blue sofa in the corner, watching with admiration as Kelly flicked on the washing machine before going over to open the oven door and baste the meat. Afterwards she rinsed the broccoli, put a lid on the potatoes, plucked some mint from the pot on the window sill and chopped it like a pro. I wanted to help, to take some of the pressure off her, but all I could do was watch.

I felt like a rubbish friend. That was just how I felt when Kelly's mum left. I hadn't really known what to say or what to do. If I'd been in her shoes I'd probably have gone to pieces, but Kelly's not like that. She coped, despite the fact that she looked fit to drop sometimes, with dark blue shadows under her eyes.

In fact, she seemed more worried about her dad and her brothers than about herself.

"Stuff her!" she said one break time, not long after her mum had left. "I'll show her that we can manage without her. In fact, I'll do better than that. I'll show her that we're better off without her around."

As I looked around the kitchen I could see that she was doing her best to live up to that promise. There was a rota attached to the fridge with jobs for the boys, the house was spick and span, and Kelly's tennis racket was still propped up by the back door, ready for use. She'd probably have had to pack that in too except for the fact that her grandma had died and left her a bit of money. She'd said that she wanted Kelly to use that money for tennis lessons. So for now, until the money ran out, she was keeping up with the tennis. I was glad.

Kelly barely showed it, but I was sure that there must have been a load of anger burning inside at the way her mum had just left them. I reckoned that running around a tennis court, smashing the ball over the net, was a good way to work it off. If I'd thought about it earlier I might even have given it a go myself. My dad hadn't even gone yet, and I was angry *and* sorry for myself despite the fact that I knew he wouldn't completely abandon us. I knew that he'd always try to be a part of our lives, if we let him.

"I'm sorry, Kelly," I murmured as she hung a selection of beautifully ironed small grey school shirts on the curtain pole above the patio door. "I'm sorry I didn't try to support you better. I'm sorry I didn't think of all the things you were having to do. I'm sorry for not being a better friend. If I could make it up to you, I would. If I had a future, I'd do something to help. I don't know what it would be, maybe just making a cake or taking the boys to the park, but I'd do something."

The trouble was, I didn't have a future. My chance to be a better friend had gone.

The back gate banged against the brick wall and made me jump. Kelly shook out her hair and smoothed her hands down over her top. She slid open the patio door.

"Hi!" she called into the garden.

It's a good thing I was sitting down or I'd have fallen over and made a complete and utter spectacle of myself. Who was kicking a football at the boys but my brother!

"Hi!" he called back, with a little wave of his hand and a strangely shy expression on his face. What on earth was he doing here? After a couple more shots at goal he loped into the kitchen.

"Anything I can do to help?"

I squinted at him. Was this an alien? Had he got a double?

"No, I'm fine," Kelly replied with a smile. "It's all done. We're ready to go."

"Hello, Mr Winterton," Jamie called through the doorway. "How are you?"

"Oh, not too bad Jamie," Kelly's father called back. "Getting there, you know."

"Good," Jamie replied. "Glad to hear it."

Kelly shook her head.

"He's not," she whispered. "I'm afraid it's a bad day today. How's Jess?"

"No change," he said, his shoulders dropping.

Kelly touched his arm briefly and he half smiled

before going outside to round up the boys.

There wasn't a lot of room in the kitchen when the chairs were pushed back from the table so I had to lift up my legs and almost lie on the sofa. The food smelled delicious and I really wished that I could tuck in as well. I even fancied that my stomach was rumbling, which was a really weird sensation. While they ate, Jamie, my normally monosyllabic brother, kept the conversation going, and when Luke knocked over his glass of juice it was Jamie who was there in an instant, mopping up with a great wad of kitchen towel and saying it didn't matter. He was being so kind and thoughtful and polite. I felt my heart swell with pride. Kelly looked pretty proud of him too. She kept shooting him little smiles of gratitude and I could see the tips of their toes touching under the table.

Afterwards, Jamie helped with the washing up and got both of the boys putting things away in cupboards while Kelly's dad went for a rest. When they were alone Jamie draped his arms around Kelly's shoulders and kissed the top of her head. It felt wrong to spy on them but I couldn't look away.

"You okay?" he asked.

"Just about," she replied, gazing up at him. "What about you?"

"Just about."

"Have you started your revision?" she asked.

He took her hand and led her towards the sofa. I leaped up, sending a cushion flying onto the floor, but they were so wrapped up in each other that they didn't notice. Jamie sat down, dropped his head into his hands and dug his fingers into his scalp.

"Aargh!" he groaned. "I've tried and tried but I just can't concentrate. My mind feels as if it's been blown to bits. All the teachers keep saying how crucial these exams are, that our futures depend on doing well at AS." He looked up at Kelly, pleadingly. "But what's more important than my sister lying in that hospital bed and nobody knowing if she's going to get better?"

Kelly twisted towards him.

"Jamie," she spoke softly but firmly, "Jess *is* going to get better, and it won't help her if you mess up your exams."

"I wish I could believe that," he said. "I wish

she'd just open her eyes and everything could go back to how it was before." His voice cracked as if he was trying not to cry. "You never know what you've got until it's gone, do you?"

Kelly rested her head on his shoulder.

"Jess hasn't gone, Jamie. You must believe that. In the same way that I believe we'll see Georgia again one day."

She lifted her head and took his face between her hands.

"I will never give up on Georgia *or* Jess and neither must you."

She planted the tenderest of kisses on his lips and he wrapped both of his arms around her, pulling her close. They looked as if they'd always belonged together. I wondered when all this had happened. Had Jamie always fancied her? Had she always liked him? How could I not have realised?

And then I was almost crying too. I managed to stifle the great big sobs that wanted to rack my body. Kelly had such faith in my recovery. I could see it in the brilliance of her eyes, hear it in the steadiness of her voice, and it was like one of those tonics Mum used to insist on us taking during the winter.

"It will make you strong," Mum used to say as she spooned the orange syrup first into Jamie's mouth and then into mine.

"Thank you, Kelly," I murmured. "Thank you so much for staying strong, for Jamie's sake. If your belief was enough to help me live then I'd be fine in no time. You said to me once that you hoped we'd be friends for life. Well, I can't manage that, I'm afraid, but maybe one day, a long time in the future, we'll meet up again in the afterlife. Take care of yourself, Kel. Don't forget me. I'll never forget you."

YASMIN

SUNDAY, 5 MARCH – 3.34 P.M.

When I was little I often used to hide behind trees in the garden or stand outside Jamie's bedroom door and spy on my brother and his friends. Now it didn't seem right and I felt like an intruder. The boys were playing on the Xbox and for a short time at least Jamie and Kelly could have some time to themselves. I left them curled up on the sofa together and set off to see Yasmin.

It was a fair walk to Yasmin's house but I was glad of it. My feet were definitely making contact with the tarmac pavements now. I could feel it – heel, ball, toe – as I strode out, and an elated energy fizzed through my invisible form.

How can I be at death's door? I thought to myself. I'm feeling better, stronger. Every time I visit someone I realise how much I want to live.

"Don't think that," I whispered to myself. "He may be listening. He may be able to hear your thoughts, sense your feelings. Keep them hidden. Bury them." I looked around in alarm, expecting Darren to make another appearance, but thankfully he was nowhere to be seen.

That didn't mean that he wasn't there though, watching me. I knew that if I wanted to see Yasmin without him intervening I had to prevent myself from thinking rebellious thoughts.

Yasmin's house isn't at all like mine. It's modern with pale, golden bricks and an up-and-over garage door the colour of fresh custard. That day it matched the daffodils which were planted in cobalt-blue pots on either side of the front porch. I remembered reading somewhere that yellow is the colour of happiness, and as I walked up to Yasmin's front door I was half happy and half scared. Would she still be the same? Secretly, I'd been worrying myself sick about her. I felt really bad about breaking my promise to walk on the night of the accident. I couldn't bear to think of her feeling guilty for the rest of her life because of my lie, my stupidity. That's why I'd left her until last. I just couldn't face up to what I might have done to her.

I walked all around the outside of the house. It looked empty. I pressed the doorbell just in case I was wrong but no one answered and I suddenly wished that I'd come here sooner. What if they'd gone away for the weekend? What if she wasn't due back until late at night and I didn't get the chance to spend enough time with her before she went to bed? What if…?

"Give yourself a break, Jess," I muttered to myself. "She'll probably have homework to do. Wherever she is, she won't want to leave herself short of time for that."

Two stone mushrooms squatted on either side of the driveway so I sat down to wait.

"Come on, Yasmin," I muttered. "Where are you? Hurry up."

It was hard to sit still. I wanted to pace up and down, backwards and forwards, over the velvety-green lawn, anywhere and everywhere, as if moving would make Yasmin miraculously appear.

"Don't wish time away," I said to myself. "Look

around you, take in all the details. After all, you'll probably never come here again as an earthly being."

Technically, of course, I wasn't 'of this world' but I didn't want to think of myself as just a spirit. I was more than that, and I wanted to at least pretend that I was part of the human race for as long as I could.

You'll probably never come here again. Such small words with such a monumental meaning. I stared down at a clump of spring daisies to the right of my feet. I loved daisies. Once upon a time, when my future had seemed to stretch out ahead of me, I had imagined sitting with Will on a lawn like this. The sun would be shining down and his face would be full of love as he made me a daisy chain and placed it gently over my head. That would never happen to me now. I studied the oblong white petals tinged with pink, their yellow pincushion centres and the minuscule, almost imperceptible hairs on the leaves.

Could you take memories to eternity? I wondered. Or maybe they'd be classed as excess baggage? In order to enter the Kingdom of Heaven with a pure heart, would you have to let go of a lot of your earthly past? It was an unbearable thought. Everything I had ever done or not done or hoped to do would just be wiped away as if it had never existed. I curled my fingers around the roughened lip of the stone mushroom and pressed my feet down against the grass. When I lifted them up there was an imprint, a definite curve from the sole of the ballet pump.

"You're still here, Jess," I said. "For now at least, you still have your dreams and memories."

I raised my gaze to see Yasmin's mum's car turn the corner at the top of the road. I could have kissed that Golf, especially when she pulled into the driveway and I saw Yasmin sitting in the passenger seat, her big brown eyes staring straight ahead, mouth set in a resigned line. Whatever the conversation had been between Yasmin and her mum, it didn't look as if it had been about the joys of spring. They both got out and began to haul a load of supermarket shopping from the boot. With every journey to and from the house Yasmin seemed to lose height. She did look smaller than I remembered. Perhaps I'd grown when I was in hospital. They say you can grow by nearly a centimetre when you're asleep at night, when gravity isn't compressing your spine. Technically, I'd been asleep for a month so it's possible that I was quite a bit taller than when I'd last seen her.

"You get the last two bags, Yasmin, and I'll put the kettle on," her mum said.

I watched as Yasmin struggled to pick up both of the bags at once. They were too heavy so she put one down by the back wheel of the car. I did what any decent friend would do: I decided to help. I wasn't sure if I'd have the strength, but at least it was worth a try. As soon as Yasmin went through the front door and along the hall I yanked the bag of tins and juice up the garden path. It wasn't nearly as difficult as I'd thought it would be.

"Wow, Jess," I said to myself, "somewhere in the last couple of days you've developed some invisible muscles. How cool is that?"

As Yasmin stepped out onto the porch I lowered the bag next to the front door. She didn't even see it. She walked straight past and back to the car. Confusion spread across her face. She scratched her head, looking behind the seats and all around

195

the perimeter of the car. Then she turned towards me and saw the bag.

"I must be going mad," she said to herself.

"Join the club," I murmured. "You think you've got problems. You want to try being me."

"You'd better go upstairs and get on with your school work," her mum said, as they finished unpacking the shopping. "Your father will be back from his conference soon. You know that he'll want to see you working."

Yasmin sighed and picked up a mug of tea. We trudged upstairs together. She was wearing black jeans and a grey top. Her long, glossy black hair fell in a plait to one side and from the back I could see the outline of her spine. The reason she looked shorter was because her shoulders were rounded and she was bent over. She looked worn down, like my mum.

Yasmin's room was ordered and still. I used to admire the way she had a place for everything. I go through phases of tidiness until the effort of it all gets too much and my room turns back into a tip. She has her own en-suite shower room, too. No sharing the bathroom with a smelly brother for her, or finding shaving stubble around the taps! The mirror above the basin glinted hypnotically, and while Yasmin got out her books I took another peek at myself. I got quite a shock.

I could see myself much more clearly. My features didn't look so much like a wishy-washy painting any more. I had colour, as if I'd lightly shaded myself in with a set of crayons. My lips were definitely pinkish, and when I looked down and slid one foot out of the ballet pump, the dancing blobs of Posh Petunia nail polish on the end of my toes looked brighter than before.

I was thrilled for a second and then the worry kicked in. Was I going to have to be more careful, to slink about like an undercover agent in case other people started to see me? Darren hadn't said this would happen. His rules hadn't extended to telling me what to do if I started to take on rainbow status. I edged to the doorway of the en-suite and looked through to the bedroom. Yasmin was seated at her desk, head bowed over a book. I moved closer. Part of me longed for her to look up.

"Hi, Jess," I wanted her to say. "How are you doing?"

I wanted it to be as if the accident had never happened and we could just pick up from where we were before.

"In your dreams, Jess," I muttered.

On the cork board above her desk she had pinned an elaborate revision timetable. I smiled. She is *so* organised and she works really hard. Yasmin's father wants her to be a doctor so she needs top grades. I think she sort of wants to be a doctor too. She likes a challenge, but on the other hand I think she'd quite like to keep her options open. She's good at music, but if I was going to choose a career for her it would be something artistic. She's an absolutely brilliant artist.

"Can I look at your latest masterpiece?" I would ask when I went round to her house.

"If you really want to," she'd say modestly, and I'd pull the big black art folder out from under her bed. I really wished I could look at it now. Suddenly, Yasmin raked her hands through her hair and let out a loud shriek.

"I can't do this," she groaned, dropping her head

on to an advanced mathematics textbook. She made me jump and I knocked against the desk. A metal cylinder full of pens flew through the air. It all seemed to happen in slow motion. Instinctively, I tried to catch them but they bounced off my fingers and landed like a pile of pick-up sticks right in the middle of the carpet.

"Oh my God," Yasmin gasped. "How on earth did that happen?"

She swivelled in her chair, eyes shifting around the room, searching for clues to solve the mystery of the ballistic ballpoints. I had the sudden urge to giggle, and I put my hand over my mouth. I don't know why I hadn't thought of it before but it suddenly occurred to me how useful being invisible could be, especially with people you didn't like. As Yasmin gathered up the pens I thought that if I'd got more time and Darren wasn't on my tail I could have visited Dad's girlfriend. It would have been nice to find out what the fascination was, and maybe make some mischief and put an atomic bomb under that relationship once and for all. Then he and Mum could get back to how they used to be. It was a brief moment of fantasy, and I enjoyed it while it lasted. In reality, I knew that life doesn't work like that.

Yasmin stayed sitting on the floor and leaned forwards to pull the artwork folder from under the bed. I sank down next to her in the middle of a fading pool of sunlight which seemed to absorb some of my colour. She'd obviously been busy while I'd been away but her style of drawing had changed. The softness had gone and it was as if the work had been yanked out of her. As she spread the still lifes, abstracts and a couple of landscapes over the carpet my mouth gaped open. I'd always known she was good but there was an extra something in those pictures, a rawness which blew me away.

Separated from the others by a sheet of pristine white tissue paper was a pastel drawing of the five of us. This was different to the other pictures. It had been copied from a photograph taken at Sara's birthday last year and it was full of bright colour and gentle lines. We all looked so happy. Who would have thought that, in the space of a few months, everything would be different?

I wondered if they missed me as much as I missed

them. How quickly would they move on? Would another girl fill the space that I would leave? I could be a bit shy and quiet sometimes, especially when everyone else was being really loud. Did that make me easy to forget? So many questions. So much hurt. It was like a knife slicing through me. I couldn't bear it. Couldn't bear the thought of letting my friends go.

"I wish I'd never done these stupid visits," I said to myself. "I thought they'd be good. I thought they'd be a nice way to say goodbye but they're not. They're just awful."

"Yasmin!"

Her father was standing in the doorway. Neither of us had heard him coming.

Uh-oh! I thought. There's trouble brewing. I could see from the way Yasmin's eyelids flickered that she was anticipating it too.

"What do you think you are doing?" he demanded.

Yasmin shoved the artwork back in the folder and pushed it under the bed.

"You shouldn't be messing about with silly

drawings when you have more important school work to get on with."

"I was just having a bit of a break," Yasmin replied, "just thinking about Jess."

You'd think that would have softened his stance, but no chance.

"I don't think you can afford to take a break, Yasmin. Your work has been slipping recently. Weren't you getting the results of that maths test today?"

She nodded, kept her head and eyes down.

Oh no! What had happened? I couldn't bear it if Yasmin's work had suffered and she was being put under even more pressure. What if her whole life path was altered because of my accident? She might not have been sure about being a doctor but she would have been a brilliant one. I had this horrible lump in my throat and a sick, hollow feeling in the pit of my stomach. Yasmin stood up and moved to the desk. I followed and stood beside her, not caring if either of them could see me. She needed protecting.

"And?" her father prompted.

"I got 89 per cent," she murmured.

Wow! 89 per cent! I thought that was fantastic.

I wanted to fling my arms around her and tell her how proud I was. From his disapproving expression her dad obviously didn't share my enthusiasm.

"And were you top of the class?" he asked.

There was silence for a moment, the tension hovering between them like an overloaded rain cloud ready to burst.

"It doesn't matter where I came in the class," Yasmin replied. "It's the grade that counts."

There was another pause. I stiffened like one of Mum's over-set jellies.

"But yes," she sighed. "If you must know, I came first."

A shred of relief relaxed the atmosphere. I didn't expect her father to come over and give her a hug. They're not a touchy-feely family like us, but I did think she deserved a smile at least. She didn't get one. I hated him in that moment, and wished that I had supernatural powers and could have struck him down with a bolt of lightning. I wanted to tell Yasmin's dad how unreasonable he was being. She worked harder than any of us. But I clenched my fists and managed to keep quiet.

"One day, Jess," I said to myself, "you're not going to be able to button that mouth of yours. One day soon someone is going to do something that forces you to blurt out what you're thinking and that really will put the cat among the pigeons."

We all knew that Yasmin's dad was pushy, but now I saw that however well she did, it would never be good enough. Even if she got 100 per cent he probably wouldn't be satisfied. It made me realise how lucky I was. Mum and Dad supported me; they wanted me to do well but they wanted me to be happy too. If I'd ever achieved 60 per cent in a maths test Dad would probably have cracked open that bottle of champagne which he kept in the fridge for special occasions. I envisaged him making some embarrassing little speech too. Suddenly I felt incredibly grateful for my dad, despite his faults.

As her father trudged back down the stairs, Yasmin gave the bedroom door a little slam. She sat back down at her desk and picked up her pen.

"You should do better, Yasmin. You'll never be a doctor if you don't come top of the class all the time. Well good," she ranted, "because I don't want to be a stupid doctor. I've never wanted to be a doctor."

When I was first taken into hospital, after the accident, I wasn't sure whether everything was real life or a dream. This felt like that. The Yasmin I knew had been adamant that she was okay with studying medicine at university.

"But if I don't get the grades," she'd said one day, "then maybe I'll still be able to get on an art foundation course."

"Yas, you'll get the grades," I'd said. "There's no doubt about that."

I sat down on her bed and lay back against the burgundy striped pillow. My head was spinning. One minute I was horrified because I thought my accident might have altered Yasmin's destiny to be a doctor and now I wondered if that was a good thing, if that was what would make her happier.

"Which university will look at a girl who gets less than 90 per cent in a maths test?" Yasmin carried on, mimicking her father's voice. "They will think you are a stupid girl and they will be right. Compared to your sister, you are not that intelligent. She will make something of her life but you will end up in the gutter."

She twisted a strand of dark hair around her finger until it curled up like one of those water snails in Gran's pond. I wanted to put my arms around her, to hold her tight and tell her it would be all right, but I didn't dare touch her. Instead, I mouthed the words I wanted to say. As I blew them across the room, a string of minuscule multi-coloured bubbles flew from my lips like particles of dust flying along the setting sunbeams.

"It's your life, Yas," I said. "If you want to go to art college instead of becoming a doctor then do it. Maybe your mum will help. Maybe she'll stand up to your dad for once. Whatever you do, don't look back with regrets."

She raised her eyes and looked over to the bed. For a second our gazes met. Could she see me? Could she feel my presence, or was I imagining, hoping? Would my words make a difference? I wasn't sure. I'd never thought that Yasmin was the sort of girl to rock the boat. She'd always seemed too obedient and I could see her, in the future, a good and caring doctor but with her real spirit elsewhere. But now I could see something else as well. It was a quality I possessed in abundance – stubbornness.

"Go for it, Yas," I whispered. "I'll try to be with you. I don't know what's going to happen to me when I die but I'm sure that I'll be somewhere, maybe on some other plane, in some other form. But wherever I am, Yas, I'll do my best to be looking out for you, to make sure that you're not alone. Remember, Yas, even when you can no longer see me, touch me, hear my voice, remember that I'm still your friend. I'll be your friend forever."

GRAN

SUNDAY, 5 MARCH – 7.16 P.M.

I left Yasmin finally settling down to her work and walked quickly in the darkness. Tomorrow was to be my last Monday on earth and I planned to spend it at school. Mum was always banging on about the benefits of a good night's sleep in term time so I decided on Gran's greenhouse as my sanctuary again.

When I pushed open the creaky little gate Gran was in the garden, taking in some washing. As she looked briefly in my direction, I melted back into the deep shadow cast by a tall conifer. After a few seconds she turned away and continued to unpeg Dad's and Jamie's shirts from the line. In profile her face was sharper, her cheeks more sunken. She looked frail. I was worried that all the help she was giving to Mum and Dad was too much for her. The back door was open and the light from the kitchen glowed enticingly onto the soft round cobbled path. I hesitated, on high alert for any sign of Darren. The night air was still, and although it was cold, there wasn't that bone-chilling iciness which seemed to precede his appearance. I knew it was against the rules, knew that I might get into trouble, but Gran seemed lonely standing there in the dark, so I couldn't resist. As she lifted the green plastic washing basket and balanced it on her hip, I nipped inside the house.

All houses smell different, but Gran's is very distinctive. The air is layered with the scent of beeswax polish, home-made lemon barley water and tapestry wool. I breathed in deeply. It was blissful. We sat together at the little round table next to the bay window while she ate her supper of boiled eggs and soldiers. I stroked the tablecloth which had been embroidered by my great-grandmother and wished I could feel Gran's elegant silver spoon balanced between *my* fingers.

I'd forgotten how relaxing her house is, how safe it feels, how the atmosphere is ingrained with her unconditional love for us. I longed to tell her how much I loved her back, to explain that I didn't love her any the less because I didn't sit on her knee any more or cuddle up for a bedtime story. Suddenly, I realised that growing up didn't have to mean growing apart. I wished I could have told her that too, but somehow I think she already knew.

After she had eaten, Gran put on a jazz CD while she ironed the shirts, spraying them with a grassy-smelling linen water to help her remove every last crease. She baked a coffee cake, Jamie's favourite, and cleaned a silver frame which contained a photo of Gramps. Finally, she moved into the sitting room to sit on the green velvet sofa and watch a detective programme on television. I lounged in the chair next to her. Time seemed to slow down. Death seemed a lifetime away.

After the news at ten-thirty, Gran made herself a hot drink and took it upstairs to bed. I followed her, but at the top of the stairs stepped into 'my room'. It was the room I always used to sleep in when I came to stay. Gran had decorated it with pink wallpaper, and there were still a couple of my teddies resting against the pillow. I hadn't slept in that bed for ages, more than a year. When we were little, Jamie and

I used to stay with Gran a lot. She'd buy us those little variety packs of cereal for breakfast and afterwards we would walk down the fields at the back of her house to the stream. Sometimes we would spot a kingfisher or rabbits, and sometimes we would catch minnows in our lime green nets and bring them back to put them in a baby bath in her garden. Once Jamie was leaning over so far that he fell into the stream, and even though the water wasn't terribly deep Gran plunged straight in after him to lift him out. She would do anything for us, my gran – absolutely anything.

I was lying on top of the bed, almost asleep, when she came in. I hadn't expected it and she didn't switch on the light. I lay perfectly still as she smoothed the quilt around its edges and drew the curtains across the window, blotting out the moon. She was in her dressing gown, holding her mug of hot chocolate, and she moved over to the corner to sit in the old button-backed chair. She sat there for ages, sipping her drink, staring into space. I wished I could work out what she was thinking. I wished I could have talked to her. After about half an hour she got up and went through to her room. As she passed close by my bed, the light from the landing lit up her face. It was wet with tears.

I didn't sleep well. Gran was up in the night. At 2.00 a.m. I heard the click of her light switch and the rustle of the newspaper. At 4.03 a.m. I awoke again as she went downstairs. There was the clink of bottles from the drinks cabinet in the dining room and I knew she was probably putting a capful of whisky into her tea or hot milk to help her sleep. It obviously didn't work because just before 6.00 a.m. I heard her running the bath. I got up and looked at myself in the mirror, expecting that my outline would be fading now. It was more than halfway through my allotted life in limbo. Surely I should be getting weaker, more haggard-looking? Surely I shouldn't look so rested and be able to see myself as well as I could?

It was a fair walk to school and still dark when I left Gran's house. For once in my life I didn't want to be late. The moon was still out, hanging beautifully in the sky like a luminous Christmas bauble. I strode out, ears pricked, eyes darting from side to side, ready for Darren, whenever he chose to appear. I had a twinge in my side, stopped, bent double, and of course he took advantage of my moment of weakness. You don't always have to see something to know it's there. There was no sound, no rustle of wings or fluttering of dried leaves as he landed but, as I watched the breath stream from my mouth like a plume of smoke, I knew he was watching.

"Go away," I gasped. "Leave me alone, can't you! I don't remember being stalked as part of the bargain."

"I'm just checking that you're all right." He sounded offended. The bite had gone from his voice but I wasn't buying it. He wasn't to be trusted.

"I'm fine. Why wouldn't I be?"

I straightened up and there he was, scarily immaculate in a starched white shirt and tight-fitting chinos, but still no shoes. He leaned back slightly and looked me up and down.

"You're making it hard for yourself, you know," he said, "and for me too."

"I don't know what you mean."

"Have you always been a bit of a rebel?"

I clasped my hand to my side. The stitch wasn't going away.

"Me? You're joking, aren't you? You're the one who called me a wimp and a scaredy-cat – remember?"

Was that only yesterday when he had flown me to Kelly's house? I was trying to pack so much into so little time. It was as if I was trying to live my whole life in the space of a few days.

He frowned.

"I know where you've been so you might as well admit it."

"Okay, I stayed at Gran's again last night, and you obviously know that I wasn't in the greenhouse. Gran looked as if she needed the company, and to be honest, so did I."

He was silent. I looked him straight in the eye.

"Go on then, beam me up. I've broken the rules again so take me back with you. It's the sixth today, isn't it? You could easily rub out a bit of the number eight and change it to a six – no one would know."

He looked horrified.

"I can't just go changing these dates willy-nilly," he said. "It wouldn't be right."

There seemed to be some sort of clockwork device whirring around in my head, like the mechanism at the back of Gran's longcase clock.

"So the other day, when I'd been home, you weren't really going to take me back and toss me in a cupboard?"

He shrugged, pushing his lips forward into an impressive pout.

"It's a last resort," he murmured. "Only to be used in an emergency."

I narrowed my eyes.

"What sort of an emergency?"

He shifted from one foot to the other, and fiddled with a strand of his hair.

"Those awkward people I've mentioned," he whispered, "the ones who get silly ideas about survival. The 'eternity escapees', we call them. They have to be rounded up."

"And how do you do that?" I asked.

He clicked his fingers and a large silver net appeared in his hand, rather like those ones that naturalists use to catch butterflies, except much larger.

"Cool!" I exclaimed, imagining him running around like the child-catcher from *Chitty Chitty Bang Bang*.

He grinned.

"Isn't it?" he said. "I haven't had to use it yet, but I can't wait."

I raised my eyebrows.

"N-not that I want you to think I'm callous or cold-hearted," he said.

"Of course not," I replied.

He twirled the net above his head like a cheerleader and shot me a sideways glance.

"Maybe I'll have to try it out on you."

I curled my toes up inside the shoes and stood very still.

"I'll make it easy for you."

"Oh, that's no fun," he said, leaning closer. "You have to run away."

The net was beside me now. One sharp movement and I'd have been entangled in its silver threadwork.

"But I really don't want to have to take you back with me yet," he said with a sigh. "It will create all sorts of complications."

With another click of his fingers the net disappeared.

"Can I tell you a secret?" he whispered. "I think it's rather nice that you went to see your gran. I was very close to my grandmother."

His eyes clouded over, turning a dark navy blue.

"I miss her a lot."

A silver teardrop appeared at the corner of one eye. I put my hand out and touched his arm. His shirt felt crisp, as if it had been freshly laundered.

"I'm sorry. Can't you go back and see her?"

He sniffed, wiped his nose with his sleeve and shook his head.

"Not as much as I'd like to. Too busy, you see. Promotion, responsibility, quotas, not enough hours in the day, all of that stuff."

"Is it worth it?" I asked. "Being an angel of death?"

He looked shocked.

"It's one of the top jobs. If you're put forward you don't turn it down."

"Why, what happens if you do? Are you condemned to shovelling coal to keep the fires of Hell going?"

He stepped back and suddenly I felt the cold radiating off him again.

 217

"It's not a joking matter," he said prissily. "I'm not sure that you're taking all of this seriously enough, Jessica."

"Oh believe me, I am," I snapped back. "Deadly seriously, and *my* time is precious too. You're holding me up."

He looked affronted.

"Where are you going now then, that's so important? I thought you'd seen all your friends?"

"I have, but not together. I'm going to school, remember? I asked your permission yesterday and you said it was okay."

"Did I?" he retorted. "Oh well, if you say so. My head is spinning from everything I have to think about. You'd better get going then. Far be it from me to hold you up."

"Fine," I said, and I began to walk.

He stayed exactly where he was, and just before I turned the corner out of sight I looked over my shoulder. He was still watching me.

SCHOOL

Monday morning had never been one of my best. Normally I was skidding into the classroom at the end of registration with some hurriedly concocted excuse. It was weird to be there in plenty of time – to be at school so early that it was still dark.

"This ought to wipe out all those detentions for lateness," I muttered.

I wanted to get inside but the high wrought-iron entrance gates were still closed.

"Waiting, waiting, waiting, that's all I'm doing at the moment," I said to myself, pressing my forehead against the peeling black paint. "I'm fed up with waiting. I haven't got time to wait, and what's a three-metre-tall pair of gates to someone who's flown over rooftops in the company of an angel of death?"

I took off my jacket to make the task easier and pushed it through the railings onto the ground where it lay waiting to cushion my fall. It was completely inadequate, of course, but it made me feel better, and before I could talk myself out of it I began to climb. When we covered the Victorians in History I'd got really bored, but as I used the twining metal stems, leaves and flowers for footholds, I was almost overcome with admiration and gratitude for their devotion to decoration. Thank goodness they hadn't discovered minimalism or I'd never have made it to the top.

"Don't look down," I said to myself as I reached the summit. But my brain just would not listen to sense and I was *so* high and the ground looked *so* far down. Little black midge-like spots swarmed before my eyes.

"Come on, Jess," I muttered. "You can't faint now. It's no higher than being at the top of a double-decker bus."

My nervous system wasn't conned by that. It's

one thing to sit on a seat protected by glass and metal and quite another to be clinging for dear life in the open air. Even if I was lighter than before *and* by some remote chance the coat softened my fall, it would still be a hard landing. Maybe I could try the flying or floating techniques that my body had insisted upon when I first came out of hospital.

Tentatively, I detached one arm from the top of the gate and then one leg. I stretched them both out so that I formed a starfish shape and then I swished them about a bit. My limbs felt heavy and definitely not in light-as-a-feather mode. Could I injure myself any more in my ethereal state? What would happen if I fell and lay across the entrance with a broken leg? No one would know I was there and all the teachers would drive their cars over me until... I clutched at the scrolled edges of the metalwork as tightly as I could, closed my eyes and fought back the drowning feeling that was rising like a spring tide. Could you die twice? It was a risk I didn't want to take. Once was proving to be more than enough.

"Okay, let's try logic," I said to myself. "Remember

Devon, a couple of years ago, how you couldn't swing yourself over the first obstacle on that assault course and how you burst into tears, unable to move one way or the other?"

"Come on, Jess." Dad's face swam behind the black dots, like an untuned TV screen. "Don't think about getting down to the ground. Just concentrate on your next foothold. Good girl. You're doing really well. Now move that hand a little to the right."

I remembered him coaxing me, willing me on, protecting me with the safety net of his love. I heard everyone clap with each small accomplishment, even complete strangers. Now I tried to dredge up that wonderful feeling, that glow of pride that had shone out of them and lit me up inside. Those people, even the ones I had never met, had given me the confidence to complete that assault course. Had it been a practice run for this? Was all of this written in my stars, even back then?

Deep breath. One leg swung over the top. There was no going back. I wobbled precariously.

"Steady yourself," I muttered. "Concentrate on your balance. Think of all those botched ballet lessons at primary school. That humiliation must have had some purpose."

I stayed, straddled, for what seemed like ages, afraid to move backwards or forwards, barely daring to blink. Was this the way it would end, impaled on top of the school gates like some grotesque mascot? This is ridiculous, I thought to myself. Normally I can't wait to get out of school, and now I'm actually desperate to get in.

There's a mirror positioned at the bottom of the drive. It's meant to help visibility when cars pull out on to the main road but it doesn't work like that if you're actually on top of the gates. Sunrise was awesome until the sun's rays struck that mirror and sent a blinding stream of light straight into my eyes. It might not seem like a blessing to be unable to see where you're going but in a strange way it helped.

"The gates will be opened soon," I told myself. "You need to get down before Alf comes and bangs them back against that concrete post."

I forced myself to find a niche for my right foot, trying to trust my instincts. There really wasn't any choice. I had to go for it. With eyes screwed shut and knuckles glowing fluorescent white from the effort of hanging on to the top rail, I shimmied over. The birds resumed their post-breakfast sing-song as if in celebration.

"Hold on a moment," I breathed. "I may be over the top but I'm not down on the ground yet."

I thought it would be easy. I thought that the worst bit was behind me, but that was tempting fate. There was a jangling of keys and Alf, the caretaker, was coming down the drive, ready to unlock the gates.

"Hang on!" I mouthed. "Just give me a minute, will you?"

But Alf wasn't picking up my message, and I clung on for dear life as he gave the gates a good push. My legs flailed against the metalwork and my mouth turned as dry as Mum's overdone shortbread. I lost my grip as the gate thudded against the stumpy concrete post, my left arm jerking through the air. I hung like a monkey in a cage but Alf was oblivious. He picked up my jacket and marched back towards the main building. When I finally got to the ground I knelt down and kissed it like the Pope. I might not have conquered my fear of heights but I had at least challenged it. In a wobbly way I felt quite proud of myself.

My sweatshirt was snagged, my leggings were smeared with green algae from the top of the gate, and my shoulder felt as if it had been wrenched out of its socket. I blew bits of conifer leaf from my clothes. I fancied I could feel my breath against my hand and my chest was definitely going in and out. I studied myself and was reminded of one of those impressionist paintings that Mum liked so much. The mix of colours was pretty to look at but I wanted – no, needed – to stay invisible. Being noticed would ruin everything. What if Mrs Baxter spotted me in class and got me doing logarithms or, even worse, page after page of geometry? What if my friends could see me? What would they do? What would I do? When would all of these questions stop? I thought that by the time you got to the brink of death all questions would be resolved. Weren't you meant to be 'at peace'? Maybe all of that was a lie, or maybe I was just different.

I zig-zagged along the drive, from shrub to

shrub, darting for cover like they do in spy films. The car park was empty so I scooted across, took up my position behind one of the brick pillars at the side entrance and waited.

Kelly was one of the first to arrive. Sometimes one of the neighbours offered to take her brothers to school, and today she bounded up the steps to the girls' changing rooms nibbling on a piece of toast, looking carefree – which just goes to show how wrong appearances can be. The teachers love her because she's always so keen, offering to put out chairs or collect in books. She doesn't deliberately suck up like some of the others but I'd often wondered why she bothered, especially when she had so many other responsibilities. Maybe school was a bit of light relief. Maybe it's different when you have a choice about doing things. Maybe if you offer to help out it takes less energy and feels more satisfying than if you shrink in a corner hoping not to be asked. At school I was the shrinking in the corner type and I was beginning to regret that now.

Kelly stashed her battered sports bag in her locker, checked her hair in the mirror and made her way up the back stairs to our classroom. It felt so strange sidling into that room behind her and seeing the table where I used to sit. She sat down and got a French sheet out of her bag, filling in some gaps in one of those passages where you have to insert the right verb. I stood behind her, watching, wanting to tell her that she'd got the tense wrong on a couple of occasions. I swallowed back the words and feelings which were welling up inside me and made a sort of glugging noise. Kelly was concentrating hard so she didn't notice, or perhaps she just mistook it for the dodgy plumbing. We had some of those big silver central heating pipes going through our classroom and they were always gurgling away.

As the classroom filled up, I moved to the back, pressing myself against the posters of the Eiffel Tower and various magazine clippings about books or trips to local exhibitions. If anyone noticed me, I was trapped at the farthest point away from the door. But no one did. As the classroom filled up everyone chatted away, oblivious of my presence. Were they all that unobservant, that lacking in intuition? Would I have been the same in their position? The answer was probably yes, and I wasn't proud of it.

Mrs Baxter bustled in with her arms full of books – the real Mrs Baxter, flesh and blood. I thought about all those maths lessons I had sat through, wishing I was somewhere else, wishing that she was somewhere else. Now I was so glad to see her as she plonked a load of textbooks on the desk. But she wasn't our form teacher. What was she doing here?

"Right," she said, clapping her hands and raising her voice. "You've got me standing in for Miss Taylor today as she's ill, and I'm not surprised looking at you lot. You're enough to wear anyone to a frazzle. What a shambles!"

She proceeded to berate several people about their untucked shirts or lack of ties. I moved towards the window and was momentarily taken aback by my reflection in the glass. It was pale and hazy like those impressions of oil slicks we got on the ham at school lunches. The sight of Nat and Sara emerging from the narrow laurel-enclosed path that ran parallel to the main drive diverted my attention. Nat's hands were moving around like a puppeteer's and her face was flushed. Distress was flaring out of her like one of those beacons they used to light in order to warn ships away from the rocks. Something was wrong.

They were arguing and Sara's face was closed off. Was it about Nat's weight? Was that the problem? I needed to know. I needed to be a part of things. I wanted to have rubbers flicked at me in History or feel my cheeks turn bright red as Mrs Baxter picked on me in Maths. Whatever it was, however bad or boring, I wanted to be there and most of all, at that moment, I wanted to know what my friends were rowing about.

"Kelly," Mrs Baxter said, standing next to her, "is there any news of Jess?"

My chest felt really full, as if it was swirling with a whirlpool of emotion.

"She's still the same," Kelly said.

"Have you been to see her yet?"

Kelly shook her head.

"We're not allowed."

"But I want you to come to the hospital," I wanted to shout out.

Mrs Baxter dropped a hand on to her shoulder.

"I'm sure Jess's parents have their reasons," she said.

Kelly nodded.

"And when she does come round, I bet you'll be one of the first people she wants to see," Mrs Baxter added.

Oh! I could have hugged her. I could have skidded across that slippery lino floor and bowled straight into her. She knew. She understood. She wasn't just a mathematical machine after all. She was human, and I actually felt a pang of sadness that she'd never know how much I'd begun to appreciate her over the last few days.

Sara and Nat walked in separately, closely followed by Yasmin. I waited for them to gather in a group, to say 'Hey, how are you?' to one another and to hug. Instead, Nat, Kelly and Yasmin exchanged some sort of coded glance and Sara sat at her desk, fiddling with her phone. We'd all had our fall-outs before but this was different. Something was really, really wrong.

Mrs Baxter called everyone together for assembly and I tagged on to the end of the line. There were some empty benches along the side of the hall so I perched on one of those and tried to absorb every detail. This was to be my last ever assembly. There would be no more wondering why the school didn't do something about the hideous faded velvet curtains on either side of the stage, no more inhaling the stench of cooked cabbage that seemed to be trapped in the walls, and no more dire singing when the music tutor chose a hymn which no one knew.

The air ebbed and flowed as everyone sat down and then rose to their feet again. They sang my favourite hymn, 'The Lord of the Dance'. That one hardly ever gets chosen, and it was almost as if someone had arranged it, as if they knew I'd be there that day. I mimed the words as usual. I hoped Darren wasn't banking on my musical abilities when I 'passed over'. There was absolutely no chance of my being selected for the Choir of Angels unless they had a splinter group that sounded like the cats' chorus!

The prayers were said right at the end, and it was true – they were praying for me. Every single person in that room bowed their head as the words were read out. It was awesome.

231

This feeling mushroomed in my chest and spread throughout my whole body. It was like being filled with sunshine, as if everyone was sending me a slice of themselves, wishing me well. I remembered an RS lesson where we'd learned about an American study of heart attack victims. Those who were prayed for had much better rates of recovery and lived for quite a lot longer than those who weren't. I had nearly a thousand people praying for me in that room alone. If it could work for those older people in the US, why couldn't it work for a fit fourteen-year-old girl in a coma in the UK? Despite everything I'd heard from the doctors and despite Darren's plans for me, at that moment I couldn't see any reason why not.

I spent the whole day in lessons. It took my mind off things. Double Maths was first, which was obviously not what I would have chosen in an ideal world but at least Mrs Baxter couldn't pick on me to answer any questions so I felt reasonably relaxed. Maybe it was the lack of pressure or perhaps it was the knock on the head that had turned me into a numerical genius, but I understood most of what she said.

It was a completely disorientating experience. Had all my previous anxiety really caused some form of mathematical blockage? Perhaps Mrs Baxter really did know something when she said I wasn't as bad as I thought. It seemed tragic that I'd go to my death finally being able to understand algebraic equations and she'd never know.

At break time we usually just wandered about. It's only twenty minutes long so there's barely time to drink some juice, eat a snack and have a catch-up. Except today was different. Yasmin went off for a music lesson, Kelly had some books to take back to the library, and Sara headed for lost property to try to track down her lab coat. Everyone seemed to be on edge and I couldn't understand why.

"What's going on, Nat?" I wanted to ask as she flicked through a magazine and slugged back a bottle of water. "Come on, I'm at death's door here. You need to be there for each other, not having some silly argument."

She bit into an apple and turned the page.

After break, Yasmin and Kelly headed for a biology lesson. When I was in the peak of health, watching them hack into a sheep's heart would be more than I could stomach, let alone now. Instead, I opted for my usual Spanish lesson with Sara and Nat. Normally we all sat in a line on the back row, Sara and me at one table and Nat on the one next door. I'd expected the two of them to sit together but they didn't. Nat sat by the window next to some guy I didn't know very well and she seemed to spend more time watching the clouds scud across the sky than concentrating on the Spanish. The whole set seemed to have progressed so quickly that it felt to me as if they'd spent the last month on the Costa Brava. If I did manage to make some miraculous recovery, would I ever be able to catch up? A void opened in my stomach. Those rogue thoughts that refused to accept the inevitable pestered me like an army of ants.

"Go away!" I demanded under my breath. "I'm not going to live so stop resurrecting my dreams."

Double English and French were before lunch and they were more comprehensible. I was amazed at how much I knew in the French vocab test and I even had the urge to answer a couple of questions in English.

"You should speak up more, Jessica," my English

teacher used to say. "You know more than you think you do."

What I didn't know was what was wrong with my friends.

"So," Kelly said as she sat down in the canteen with a large plate of sausage and mash, "have you spoken to her?"

Yasmin was tucking into a cheese and pickle sandwich and a bowl of chips. Nat had just peeled the top off her Tupperware container which was only a third full of the predictable salad. I sat beside them and could swear I was salivating – not for the salad, though.

"I've tried," Nat said, spearing a quarter of tomato. "She doesn't think she's doing anything wrong."

Kelly sucked in her breath.

"I don't think Jess would be of that opinion."

Me? What about me? What *were* they talking about? Sara wasn't there so it was obviously something to do with her. I scanned the other tables and looked to see if she had joined the end

235

of the queue over by the serving hatch, but she was nowhere to be seen.

"Sara won't change her mind," Yasmin added. "You know how stubborn she can be."

"I'm sorry," Kelly said. "I don't care what excuses she comes up with, it's not right. When Jess finds out…"

She paused. There was a sudden stillness around our table. I knew exactly what Yasmin and Nat were thinking. They might not have been saying it out loud but it was definitely going through their heads: that I probably wouldn't get the chance to find out whatever it was they were discussing.

"Well…" Kelly continued. "I wouldn't want to be in Sara's shoes. Call herself a best friend? She's not the sort of friend I want if she goes ahead with this."

"Me neither," Yasmin added.

"Maybe she won't do it," Nat said. "Maybe when it comes down to it, she'll think of Jess and how she would feel."

She twirled a piece of lettuce around on her fork.

"I dreamed about her the other night," she said, softly. "It was so weird, as if she was in the room with me."

She put down her fork and tears trickled down her cheeks.

"I miss her so much. Now she's gone I realise how important she was to us. She held us together when we had silly rows and she was always so thoughtful, organising get-togethers or remembering when someone had a big test coming up. I want her back here, back with us, back where she belongs. I want to tell her how special she is."

I put my hands to my mouth.

"I am here, Nat," I whispered through my fingers. "I want to tell all of you how special you are too."

I longed to put my arm around her, and I would probably have thrown caution to the wind and done it too but Kelly got there first.

"We all want her back," Kelly said. "And she will be soon. I'm sure of it. When she's well we'll have a big party in my garden with balloons and chocolate cake and fairy lights strung in the trees."

Sometimes people think more of you than

you realise and sometimes people mean more to you than you really know. The truth can be bittersweet. It can come too late. What do you do when someone has so much faith in you? Do you let them down or do you try to live up to it? I knew what you should do. The trouble is *should* and *could* may sound alike, but in reality they're worlds apart.

They changed the conversation after that – tried to lighten it by talking about films they wanted to see, books they'd read, boys they fancied. I wanted to take part in a listening sort of way but I couldn't. All I could think about was Sara and what she had done to upset them.

I've always found it difficult to concentrate during afternoon lessons. By then the fluorescent lights are making my head fuzzy and my limbs heavy, but Monday afternoons were the exception. We had Food Tech, and although I'll never make a Cordon Bleu chef, it was always fun. Sara and Kelly were in my group and normally the three of us worked together. It was pretty obvious that the two of them didn't want to pair up today but everyone else was sorted so there wasn't a choice. Today the class were making a lemon meringue roulade, which sounded delicious. Mrs Cook (no kidding!), our teacher, had stressed the dangers of grease when whisking egg whites and Kelly whizzed a cut half of lemon around her bowl to ensure that her meringue was as impressive as a cumulonimbus cloud. Sara looked as if she was on another planet. *I* was more of a presence in that lesson than she was. Kelly leaned over the table and offered the cut lemon to Sara.

"What's that for?"

"To make sure your whites whisk up."

"Why shouldn't they?" Sara's shoulders were jumping up around her ear lobes.

"Weren't you listening?" Kelly asked.

"Of course I was," she snapped back. "You think you're so much better than me, don't you?"

Whoa! I thought. Where did that come from?

"Course not," Kelly replied. She sounded taken aback at the viciousness of Sara's tone. "I just don't agree with what you're doing, that's all."

What, whisking up her egg whites without a lick of lemon in the bowl? Surely that wasn't what she meant?

"Someone whose mum can't keep her legs together isn't in a position to lecture me," Sara bit back.

I gasped.

That was totally out of order. Kelly's face twitched with pain. Mrs Cook looked over.

"Everything all right, girls?"

"NO!" I wanted to shout. "Come over here and sort this out. Wipe away those evil words with an anti-bacterial lashing of your tongue." But Kelly and Sara just nodded in reply and moved slightly apart from each other. At our work station the rest of the lesson passed in silence.

"That looks lovely, Kelly." Mrs Cook beamed at the roulade as everyone else washed up their tins and put away their stuff. "Your family should enjoy that."

Kelly managed a faint smile. In the background Sara glowered, and I knew it wasn't just because her roulade had turned out to be a gloopy mess. She hadn't even bothered to put it in a tin to take home but just dumped it straight in the bin. As Kelly walked across the room to put her perfect pudding in the fridge I had a premonition that something bad was about to happen. The moment I saw Sara's leg begin to swing backwards I was there in an instant. Without a second thought I kicked her in the shin, as hard as my flimsy foot could manage. I really didn't expect it to have much of an effect. When she shouted out it even made me jump.

"Ouch!" she shrieked.

As Kelly half tripped I was there to catch the roulade, to stop her *and* it from falling. For that split second nobody was looking at us. They were all concentrating on Sara.

Serves you right, I thought as she bent over to rub her shin. Maybe that'll teach you not to be so mean.

I didn't know what had got into her. She wasn't usually like that at all.

Betrayal

Monday, 6 March – 4.00 p.m.

Sara usually calls in at her gran's after school on Mondays so I thought we could walk together, probably for the final time. I waited at the top of the drive and watched my friends walk past me – Nat, Yasmin, Kelly, all off to lead their lives. I blew them kisses and waved, watching them walk down between the trees until I could no longer see even the tops of their heads. I collapsed to a crouching position and shuddered as great silent sobs took over my unearthly form.

Nearly everyone had left, and as I regained my composure I wondered if Sara had gone past without me noticing. I was just about to wander back up to the classroom when she came sashaying around the corner from the changing rooms. She looked fabulous. Her hair was loose and she'd obviously had subtle layers cut into it over the weekend.

To be honest, I felt a bit miffed that she could be thinking about such trivialities when I was lying dying *and* she hadn't even tried to sneak her way in to the hospital to see me – but hey, life has to go on.

She was my best friend, and it seemed mean to begrudge her the odd treat. In a crisis some people drop and some shop, and I reckoned that Sara was just doing her best to cheer herself up in the midst of her despair. She had some new clothes too: great jeans with a sparkly belt and a fitted top which emphasised her figure. Around her neck was a tiny crystal pendant in the shape of a star and her eyelashes were loaded with mascara. She'd obviously done a good job of avoiding the teachers after transforming herself from schoolgirl to sophisticate and I was pretty sure that she hadn't made all that effort for her gran. She had to be meeting a boy. I felt a frisson of excitement and hoped he was kind, caring and patient. In less than two days I was going to meet my maker and Sara would need someone to support her.

We caught the bus into town. The central shopping area was heaving with people who'd come straight from school or college and the air seemed to buzz with a sort of static electricity. Maybe it was that or maybe it was being with Sara, but I felt a real lift in my energy levels. It was a good thing too. She was skitting up and down escalators, rifling through rails of clothes, browsing over state-of-the-art mobile phones. She didn't buy anything and I tried not to get distracted in case I lost her, but the shops were full of floaty, summery things that stroke your skin and make you feel light and happy. I checked the price of a bright pink silk top with little bronze studs around the edge. It was far too expensive but it would be just the thing to wear at that party that Kelly was planning for me, the party that I would never get to attend. As if to emphasise the hopelessness of my situation, Sara checked her watch for the umpteenth time.

We wove through the market, inbetween stalls spilling over with fruit and vegetables, and headed down one of the narrower lanes into the oldest part of town. I cursed the thin soles of the yellow ballet pumps as the uneven cobbles gave me an impromptu dose of reflexology. Sara stopped outside her favourite gift shop and checked her watch yet again. Normally she drove us all mad with her habit of being the world's worst time-keeper and I felt slightly irritated. I really didn't need reminding of the minutes ticking by, especially not by my best friend. She obviously decided that she'd got time to spare, so she pushed open the door to the shop and headed straight for the birthday cards. I followed her inside.

"Of course, Nat's birthday is next week," I said softly to myself, a horrible thought causing my hands to fly up to my mouth. Mum and Dad might arrange my funeral for that day. I couldn't allow that to happen, so there and then I decided to disobey Darren yet again. I would have to go home one more time. If I left a note on my bedside table or wrote something in Mum's kitchen diary, at least they'd know to avoid the sixteenth and at least I'd have spared Nat the cruelty of having her birthday spoiled for evermore.

Sara headed straight down the stairs into the basement and picked up various items, turning them over in her hands. She never could resist touching things – it used to drive her mum spare when we were little. Some silk butterflies cascaded down on a string from the ceiling. She twiddled with them absent-mindedly.

"No, not those," I mouthed. "Nat's scared of things that flutter. You should know that."

Sara wasn't listening. We were so close, almost like sisters, that I thought she'd have picked up my messages but she was too preoccupied, as if she didn't really want to be doing this, as if she was just killing time. How I hated those words all of a sudden, and yet hadn't I done that plenty of times myself, *killed time*? What a waste.

A variety of embroidered bags nestled on a low shelf. They were just Nat's sort of thing. I nudged one towards the edge and Sara's eyes settled on it. Result! Except she picked up a packet of butterflies and walked towards the stairs. What *was* the matter with her?

"Listen to me," every cell in my body resonated. "That is not the right present for Nat. You're normally so good at this sort of thing."

She didn't falter, and despite Darren's earlier ticking off, I really couldn't see the harm in a little interference. I picked up the bag and lobbed it at her. It was a pretty good throw and hit her right between the shoulder blades. She gasped, dropped the butterflies and tripped up the bottom step. The assistant came dashing down the stairs with a health and safety expression firmly fixed to her face.

"Are you all right?" she asked.

"Yes, fine." Sara's voice was a bit wavery. "I'm not sure what happened."

I kicked the packet of butterflies under a set of bookshelves cluttered with bits and pieces.

"This bag is lovely, isn't it?" the assistant said as she retrieved it from the floor. "Is it a present? I can wrap it for you, if you like?"

"Well, actually I was going to get something else," Sara replied.

My frustration levels hit the ceiling and bounced off the walls. I wondered if telepathy featured heavily on the heavenly curriculum. I hoped so, because I was obviously desperately in need of lessons. Sara checked her watch again. Whoever this guy was he must be pretty important,

I thought. Obviously she didn't want to be a second late, but then she probably didn't want to turn up early either and look too keen.

"Actually, perhaps the bag *will* do," she said. "I'll take it."

Hurray! I almost said it out loud.

She wasn't bothered about having the present gift-wrapped and she fidgeted while the assistant carefully counted out her change. I followed Sara out of the shop, fizzing with curiosity. In my wildest, worst dreams I couldn't have predicted what was about to happen.

Sara didn't look. She just stepped off the kerb, almost into the path of a dark green car. Instinctively, I flung out my arm and she smacked into it, jerking backwards.

"What the…?"

The wing mirror must have missed her by a millimetre. I was shaking. So was she but she recovered more quickly, crossing the road and hurrying up Cathedral Lane. Only someone who knew her well would detect the slight tremor in her gait.

"You stupid, stupid girl," I muttered.

How could she be so careless, so thoughtless? Surely one of us being pulverised was more than enough. Hadn't my accident taught her anything?

I caught up with her just by the posh restaurant where Dad took Mum a couple of years ago on their wedding anniversary. Sara stopped in the doorway and fished a compact mirror out of her bag. It had a preening diamanté cat on the front and I'd given it to her last Christmas. We'd had a good chuckle when she unwrapped it. Even she had admitted the cat looked a bit like her. Now, she brushed away a few loose specks of mascara and re-applied some lip gloss before glancing at her full reflection in a pane of glass. She dipped her chin and shook her head to fluff out her hair.

"You look great, Sara," I whispered. "He's a lucky guy."

She smiled at herself, as if she was pleased with what she saw, adjusted her posture, took a couple of deep breaths and strode up to the tea shop two doors away.

The windows were slightly steamed up but someone behind the glass raised their hand

and waved. Sara tilted her head coyly to one side and twiddled her fingers back in the same direction. As the door opened and she flounced inside I caught sight of him. It was as if I was paralysed, unable to drag my gaze away, even though I couldn't bear to watch. Will half stood up. He smiled that endearing lopsided smile, the one that I had kidded myself was really only meant for me. Sara simpered. It was nauseating, heart-breaking.

I should have walked away there and then, left them to it, but I couldn't. I didn't even have the energy to move inside, sit at the next table and create an icy atmosphere, or tip the oil and vinegar, which sat on a nearby shelf, into her lap. All I could manage was to totter to the side and press my face to the outside of the window. Maybe I'd made a mistake? Maybe it wasn't what it looked like at all?

They ordered a pot of tea to share. Sara doesn't even like tea. Will had a buttered teacake and she leaned over, playfully tearing a little bit off the edge and popping it into her mouth. Ugh! No mistake. She was blatantly making a move on him. How despicable was that when she knew exactly how I felt?

We'd spent ages sitting in the garden or lying on my bed dreaming up ways for me to get closer to him, fantasising about the dates he'd take me on, even the wedding we'd have!

Now I understood what my friends had been so mad about at school. Somehow, they knew what Sara was up to. Maybe she'd told them, but I didn't think so. It was more likely that Will had told Jamie he was meeting up with Sara and my brother had passed the news on to Kelly. Was this their first meeting or had they been dating for weeks? Had Sara made a play for Will the minute I was in hospital and out of the way? I tried to remember if she'd ever shown any interest in him when they'd met at my house. Had their hands brushed accidentally as they passed in the hall or their eyes met over a glass of orange squash in the garden?

"Get a grip, Jess," I murmured. "You've read too many of those romantic short stories in Gran's magazines."

I was transfixed as Will looked down at his teacake, seemingly studying each remaining currant. I tried to interpret every blink of his eyelids, every thought passing behind the fixed expression on his face. Did he look a bit embarrassed or was I imagining it? Sara leaned towards him, their heads almost touching across the table. It was horribly compulsive viewing. Will tends to mumble sometimes and I'm rubbish at lip-reading, but if she'd been sitting on his knee she couldn't have paid closer attention to his words. Part of me longed to push open that door and plonk myself at the next table so that I could hear exactly what they were saying to each other. But I didn't dare.

"Don't, Jessica," I mumbled. "Don't put yourself through any more pain."

It was bad enough watching as she made Bambi eyes at him without hearing them whisper sweet nothings to each other. She placed her hand over his. He shook his head and pulled it away. It should have given me hope but his reaction was too slow. If he really objected to the way she was behaving, why didn't he raise his voice, look angry and storm out?

Just when I thought it couldn't get any worse, Will stood up to leave. They hadn't been there that long and Sara looked a bit put out but she soon recovered.

Instinctively I knew what she was going to do. My fingers flew halfway across my eyes as she stretched up on tiptoes, touched Will's navy-blue T-shirt with her fingertips and kissed him full on the lips. Okay, he might have looked a bit surprised, but he didn't exactly resist. I was in meltdown. My best friend and the boy I was secretly in love with had betrayed me, and the facts slammed into me as hard as I'd hit that car.

Betrayal's first friend is disbelief. I'd already learned that when I found out about Dad's affair. I hadn't wanted to believe that he could be so fickle, that Mum, Jamie and I didn't matter enough for him to resist temptation. Now, despite the tsunami of sorrow that was threatening to drown me, I didn't want to accept what I was seeing, but I had to.

I felt like such an idiot, as if everything Sara and I had done together over the years was a lie. She didn't really care about me. How could she, or she wouldn't behave like this? I thought we'd be there for each other, through good times and bad, protecting each other, respecting each other, for as long as we lived. It was an unspoken code, and now I realised that it was as fickle as her friendship. How could I have been taken in by it all?

"Because you trusted her, Jess," I whispered to myself. "Because you know, better than you have ever known anything else in your short life, that you would never, ever have done the same to her."

I clutched my stomach, which felt as if it contained a barbed-wire ball of anger. Suddenly I didn't want to be polite, well-mannered Jessica any more, always biting her lip, never making much of a fuss. I wanted, just once, to let rip. So I did. I clenched my fists and I banged on that window, thumped so hard I saw the glass tremble. They sprang apart. A spark of satisfaction burned inside me. People stopped in the street, staring. I didn't care whether they could see me or not. I carried on banging, thud, thud, thud, like the tolling of the funeral bell.

"You won't get away with this," I thwacked through the glass at Sara. "I'll haunt you for the rest of your days. I'll never forgive you. You couldn't even wait till I was dead."

A siren blared in the distance, and brought me

back to the street where crowds were beginning to gather. I ignored the gasps and screams as I pushed my way through them and, despite the weak feeling in my legs, I ran. Anywhere. Just away from that place, away from Sara and Will, but I couldn't outrun my thoughts and the sight of them kissing. I didn't think that I'd ever trust anyone ever again, on earth or in heaven.

Family

There's only one place you want to be when your world has fallen apart and that's home.

Dad's car was parked outside and, as I sneaked in through the open utility-room door, the smell of braising steak and onions spilled out of the kitchen. It's Dad's speciality dish. In fact it's the only thing he can really cook, and he doesn't do that very often.

As he stood by the oven I longed to throw myself into his arms, sob against his chest and pour out what Sara had done to me. I wanted to feel his kisses on the top of my head as he murmured that I wasn't to worry, that everything would be all right. But I couldn't do any of that. Instead I sat at the table and watched him as he stirred and seasoned, set out two place mats and arranged cutlery. In the place where I would have sat he placed a small jug of miniature daffodils from the garden. The curtains were drawn against the darkness, steam curled up from the saucepan of potatoes and slowly I began to feel calmer.

Mum was obviously doing the evening shift with me at the hospital so Dad plated up some supper and put it in the bottom oven to keep warm.

After he and Jamie had eaten, we all went through to the sitting room and watched an old war film on DVD. They must have played that film umpteen times over the years but it was as if they were watching it for the first time. Before the accident I'd have huffed and puffed about it but now, snuggled up in my favourite chair, listening to them swap bits of historical information, I felt reassured. So much seemed to have changed in my short time away, it was good to see that some things had stayed the same. Mum got back at about ten o'clock. Dad leaped up the minute he heard her key in the lock.

"Everything okay?" he asked, helping her off with her coat.

Her face was white and drawn. I could see lines that hadn't been there a month ago.

"Yes. She's the same. Except..."

"What?"

Dad's question was faster than a bullet from one of those guns in the film he'd been watching.

"I don't know." Mum shook her head. "I just wondered tonight, just had a feeling that something had changed."

"For the worse?"

The house seemed to be holding its breath. I clutched at the banisters.

Mum looked up at him, her eyes shining with tears. She shook her head.

"I was talking about that last holiday we had in Spain, and I just had the feeling that she could hear me."

"Did she move?"

Dad stretched out and held on to the top of Mum's arms, his fingers gently curving around the Liberty fabric of her shirt.

"No," Mum said softly. "But she's different. I told one of the nurses and she just looked at me with pity in her eyes. But I'm her mother. I know these things."

She looked up at Dad.

"Am I being silly? Was I imagining it?"

"Yes, you are imagining it, Mum," I whispered, but Dad disagreed with me. He shook his head and wound one arm right around her, stroked the nape of her neck with his other hand. He laid his cheek against hers.

"No, you're not being silly. Those doctors and nurses don't know our Jess like we do. She's a fighter. She won't give up."

Darren was waiting for me in my bedroom, hiding behind the door.

"Oh! You made me jump," I gasped.

"Serves you right," he replied. "What did I tell you? You're not allowed here. It's against the rules *and*—" he raised his eyebrows so high they almost touched his halo, "you've been interfering. I could forgive the birthday present. Your friend, whatever her name is, might have picked up the bag anyway, but the roulade that was about to go splat?" He sighed deeply. "*That* was more of a major meddle."

I sat down on the bed.

"Well, what was I meant to do? Sara was being an utter cow."

"Yes, she was, but I've told you before that you're not allowed to get involved. Anyway, I thought she was your best friend?"

"She is – was," I muttered.

He sat down next to me.

"Didn't I say that it would be interesting, your invisible visit?"

I didn't reply. 'Interesting' was not the word I would have used. 'Devastating' would have been more appropriate.

"So, what am I going to do about you being here, disobeying the rules again?" he asked.

I stayed silent.

He looked around my room.

"This is nice and cosy. I can see why you want to come back here. I love the curtains. Did you choose this fabric yourself?"

"Yes."

"You've got better taste in soft furnishings than you have in clothes."

"Thanks very much!"

He got up and wandered over to Samantha's cage and wiggled his finger through the bars.

"Cute," he said as she poked her nose out of the igloo.

There were some photos on my dressing table: Mum and Dad in happier days, Gran and Gramps, and a big picture of all my friends taken on a day trip to Alton Towers. He sauntered over and picked that one up.

"You've got lots of people rooting for you, Jessica Rowley."

"I know."

"You're a lucky girl."

Was he trying to make me even angrier than I already felt?

"In not much more than twenty-four hours I'm going to die. That doesn't feel very lucky to me."

He put the photo down in exactly the same place and studied his nails.

"No, I suppose not."

"Don't you find your job rather depressing?" I asked.

261

"It shouldn't be," he replied. "I'm meant to be taking you to a better place."

"What do you mean 'meant to be'?"

My voice was a bit high-pitched. Alarm crept over me like a swarm of ants prickling at my skin.

"Isn't it better where I'm going?"

"Oh yes, it's lovely," he reassured. "I suppose it's because I'm a bit new to it all that I sometimes find it difficult. The more experienced angels try to prepare you for all of that but..."

"How new?" I interrupted.

"Oh, don't worry, not brand new. I do know what I'm doing. I started gathering people up after Christmas and I did a lot of theory before that."

"I don't suppose it helps when you have someone like me," I said.

"No."

He looked thoughtful.

"Actually, you're the youngest person I've had to deal with so far. I'd heard the young ones could be 'fighters'."

I turned and looked at him, his knees pressed together, wings neatly folded in.

"I'm sorry," I said. "I don't mean to be difficult. It's just really hard to accept – the death thing."

He nodded.

"How did you end up doing this? Weren't there other job opportunities?" I asked.

"I sort of drifted into it. But it's fine."

A defensive note had suddenly crept into his voice. He looked at my bedside table.

"Is that clock right? I shall have to go. I've got an appointment on the other side of town."

He stood up and looked down at me.

"I'll see you tomorrow. Don't be late."

"What about now?" I asked. "What shall I do? Where shall I go?"

He shook out his wings and adjusted his halo.

"Oh I don't know. I suppose you might as well stay here. It can't do too much harm at this stage."

And he was gone, leaving a little whirlpool of air in the middle of my room and a downy white feather on my carpet.

Sleep and confusion don't go together. This would be my last ever night in my own bed, my last few precious hours with Samantha. I wanted to be calm but adrenaline seemed to be surging through my body. Dad's words, "She's a fighter", ran around inside of me as if they were on a conveyor belt, getting faster and faster.

I'm good with words, even if I don't like speaking up in class. Essays have never been a struggle and spelling seems to come naturally. Mum says that I talked before I walked, but until I was in the coma, until the power of speech was taken away from me, I took words for granted. They were just there, zipping around inside me, absorbed by my eyes and my ears and flying out from my lips. All those messages passing from my subconscious to my conscious and back again, and for most of the time I hadn't really paid much attention. *She's a fighter.* They were just someone else's words inside my head. Or were they more than that, and was it too late to listen to them?

Pretty much all my life I'd done as I was told but that night disobedience had the upper hand.

Fight, Jess. You don't have to accept your fate. Think. There must be some way out of this.

I thought about Kelly and Nat and Yasmin and how I wanted to be with them. I thought about Mum and Dad, Gran and Jamie, and how much I loved them. I even thought about Mrs Baxter. She wasn't so bad after all.

I tried not to think about Sara but of course she was there, in the background, all the time. As I lay back on my pillow and closed my eyes it was as if her face was right in front of me. She started off looking her normal sweet self with that generous smile and open attitude but then she morphed into someone unrecognisable with grotesque make-up and a mocking expression. She was sinking her talons into Will, snatching him from right under my nose. How could she do this to me? She shouldn't be allowed to get away with it. It wasn't fair! I wanted to be able to say something to her face. More than that, I wanted revenge. I knew it was wrong but I just couldn't help myself. Briefly, I wished she could die instead of me.

When I finally dropped off to sleep it wasn't surprising that I had a nightmare.

I was in the car with Mum, Dad and Jamie.

I'm not sure where we were going, maybe to do the supermarket shop. We were heading down that depressing road Dad hates on the way to the retail park. Jamie was listening to music on his iPod and I was sending a text to Gran. She's still a novice at texting so I try to give her plenty of practice. Out of the corner of my eye I saw Dad repeatedly glance in his rear-view mirror. I turned around to see what was distracting him.

A hearse, waxed and polished to perfection, was advancing fast towards our tail. As it got closer I could see the driver. It was Darren, a black silk top hat rocking precariously on his head. Beside him sat a vicar with wild grey hair and mesmerising eyes. Behind them both was the coffin. I was transfixed. The hearse got closer and closer until it was almost touching our bumper. By now Mum had turned in her seat.

"That's in a hurry," she said to Dad. "Slow down, so it can go past."

But the hearse didn't want to go past, and as I watched the vicar leaned forward and beckoned slowly towards me with his finger.

Dad had put his foot down on the accelerator and I was aware of our car pulling away. As it did so I caught sight of the number plate and I started to shake uncontrollably. My initials were on the front of that hearse.

Even Jamie sensed that something was going on. Dad was up to 80 miles per hour now in a 50-mile limit. We were weaving in and out of cars and jumping red lights. I had faith in him, that he could get me out of this, but whatever Dad did, wherever he went, that hearse stuck to our bumper like superglue. We approached the big roundabout that joined the motorway and I knew that, at that speed, even Dad wouldn't be able to control the car. I put my hands over my eyes and prepared for the crash.

I awoke with a jerk. I was on the floor, all of the breath knocked out of me. I dragged myself to a sitting position but I was dizzy and disorientated. I looked at the clock, the numbers swimming in and out of focus. It was 00.01 on Tuesday, 7 March, exactly twenty-four hours away from my demise.

"This time tomorrow," I murmured, "I am going to die.

267

"Don't pass out," I repeated over and over again, gripping the sides of the bed.

"Keep calm. Have faith in yourself. You're a fighter."

There was a galloping feeling in my heart space; faster and faster it went. I crossed my hands over my chest but still there was this pounding and pulsating against my palms. It was as if my invisible heart was about to explode into smithereens, and then surely both my lives would be over.

"NOT YET!" I shouted. "It's not fair. It's not time."

The door to my room burst open and slammed back against the wall. I heard the little silver mirror that I'd put there just before the accident shatter into a myriad of pieces.

I wondered if you could get seven years' bad luck where I was going. Jamie stared around the room but he didn't come in. His hair was ruffled from sleep and he looked about five years old.

I stayed very still, trying to regulate what little breath I had left, hoping he wouldn't notice the rumpled duvet and different books on my bedside table. My heart calmed and my vision cleared.

It seemed to have just been a panic attack.

He walked over to the guinea-pig cage and checked Samantha's door was closed. He trailed his fingers across my bookshelves and fiddled with a couple of ornaments on the top shelf before looking all around the room.

"Don't die, Jess," he gulped. "Please don't die."

"I'll try not to, Jamie," I mouthed silently. "I don't know how I'll get out of it, but I'll do my very best. I promise."

REFLECTION

TUESDAY, 7 MARCH – 8.35 A.M.

It was eight thirty-five when I woke up the next morning. I lay under my duvet and watched my clock as the second hand went around and around. Was it my imagination or was it going faster than normal? Had an hour become half an hour, a minute become thirty seconds? I reached out and placed the clock facedown on my bedside table.

Sunshine flooded into my bedroom, birds sang in the beech tree outside and a gentle breeze threaded through the slightly open window, stirring the sawdust at the bottom of Samantha's cage. It was a beautiful day, the sort that makes you glad to be even half alive. I brushed my hair very gently, avoiding the scar on the back of my head, and applied some mascara.

"I've got one day left, Sam," I said, as she dozed

in her little igloo. "I want to make the most of it. If you're lucky someone will put you out in your run later."

Downstairs, Dad was tidying away the breakfast things while Jamie stuffed books in his tatty old bag and told Dad not to stress about him being late for school because he'd got a free period first thing. Mum had woken up with a migraine and was still in bed. As Jamie crashed out of the back door I followed Dad upstairs.

I looked around my parents' bedroom. Mum had photographs on her dressing table too: a picture of their wedding day, Gran and Gramps on holiday, Jamie and me in the paddling pool when we were small. In front of those was a clay pot that Jamie had made when he was about six and above the bed hung a picture of a robin which I'd painted in Year One.

"Just nipping into the office briefly before I go to the hospital," Dad said, straightening the duvet and kissing Mum on the cheek. "Is there anything you need?"

She didn't open her eyes. Just shook her

head, almost imperceptibly. Tears glistened on her eyelashes.

He sat on the edge of the bed.

"Do you want me to stay?"

"No."

A whisper of a word, so unconvincing.

"There's no one with Jess. I'll be all right."

"So will I, Mum," I mouthed. "You can leave me for a little while, you know."

Dad kissed her again and buried his face in her hair. Guilt oozed out of his pores. Could he feel all of the hurt he had caused her? Was remorse caught up in his embrace? I liked to think so and I hoped that he meant it.

After Dad left I sat in the quietness, watching Mum, listening to her breathing. She might have been half-hidden under the covers, her head buried into the pillow to still the pain, but I didn't need to see Mum to feel her love for me. She left a trail of it wherever she went. We'd only had fourteen years together, nearly fifteen if you're counting from conception, but I could have sat there for the longest of lifetimes and not been able to return her devotion to me. I tried though, and

I knew that, whatever happened, wherever I went, our love for each other would never end.

I also tried to imagine how she felt looking at me in that hospital bed, pouring her love into me, willing me to get better. She'd stroked my hand day after day, and once she'd sobbed that she wished it was her lying there instead of me.

I scrunched myself up in the pink velvet chair next to Mum and Dad's big double bed and dug my nails into my scalp. If I felt only a fraction of her distress it was too much. I wanted to be strong for her, so that if she'd been able to see me in my invisible life, she'd have been proud of me. She was lying there, with no idea that there were less than twenty-four hours to go before her beloved daughter was to die. Gran says that ignorance is bliss sometimes but part of me wanted to warn Mum of what was about to happen. I thought it might make things easier for her.

"Don't be stupid, Jess," I said to myself. "You know it doesn't work like that."

We'd known for ages that Gramps was going to die, but when he did I still wasn't ready, still couldn't believe that he had gone. Now I needed some space.

"Sleep tight, Mum," I said, kissing the ends of my fingers and resting them a centimetre away from the top of her head. "I hope you feel better soon. I'll see you later."

The sun may have been shining but it looked cold outside, so I went back through to my room, grabbed my turquoise beret to cover my head and rummaged in my chest of drawers for the grey scarf with the silvery sequins down one side. Sara had bought it for me last Christmas and she must have tried it on before giving it to me because there was the faintest hint of her perfume nestling in the fibres. I crumpled it up into a ball and hid it away where I couldn't see it. Instead I picked out a scarf printed with summer flowers and looped it around my neck. Finally, I grabbed an old purple coat from the wardrobe and leaned into the cage to kiss Samantha on the tip of her snuffly little nose.

I meandered through the suburbs, lingering outside my old junior school and remembering the fun we'd had playing tag during break, the treat of lessons held outside under the cedar tree in the summer and the long corridor lined with a selection of our artwork.

I strolled past the little parade of shops where Mum bought our fruit and veg, daily newspapers and guinea pig food. Every couple of weeks she used to treat us to a cake from the bakery. My favourite was a deep blackcurrant tart topped with a swirl of whipped cream. Jamie always went for something chocolatey, while Dad had a lemon iced bun and Mum chose a millefeuille. Whatever had been going on at home Mum always bought four cakes, a statement that we were still a family, still together. I used to think that when there were only three cakes in the box it would mean she had given up on Dad. I never thought she'd be buying one less cake for a different reason. Perhaps Mum wouldn't be able to come to terms with it either. Perhaps she'd just stop going to the bakery and buying cakes at all.

I walked past the end of the cul-de-sac where Dad had taught me to ride my little pink bike without the stabilisers. The road is quiet, without many parked cars, so I could wobble and weave away to my heart's content. I'd been in such a hurry to get rid of those stabilisers and catch up with Jamie. Now I wished I hadn't been so at home on two wheels; perhaps then I'd have walked to Yasmin's on the day of the accident or if I'd taken the bike I'd have been more cautious and not travelling so fast. Then I'd have had time to stop before hitting the car. Mum had taken me for riding lessons when I was little but I'd never been a horsey person. If I hadn't got the hang of riding a bike either I'd probably still have been living my humdrum life, bored by school and with no idea at all of how lucky I was just to be alive.

Farther down from that cul-de-sac is the bowls club where Gramps used to play. The gates are always locked, but as I sauntered past something moved behind the hedge. My stride faltered slightly.

"Gramps?" I called softly. "Is that you?"

There was no answer and I quelled my disappointment.

"You were lucky to see him once," I said to myself. "Don't be greedy."

On the other side of the road is the church where our school carol service is held. I punched the button on the pedestrian lights and waited. A chill ran down my spine, as if someone had dropped an ice cube down my back. I turned. There was no one nearby but I felt sure I was being followed.

"Get a grip, Jessica," I said sternly as my stomach started to bubble with nerves. "He won't do anything to you yet. You've got a deal and he's stuck to it so far, hasn't he? Besides, he won't want to strike you down in public."

I pushed against the heavy oak door to the church and stepped into safety. The scent of narcissi and the splashes of stained glass welcomed me. I tiptoed past the font and slid onto a chair smooth as glass from generations of worship. From behind I could feel the gaze of the stone angels who guarded the bell tower and my hands automatically clasped themselves together.

As I stared down at the parquet floor, my thoughts began to flow. In no particular order, some of the things I would miss floated through my brain: having my ears pierced, mastering the guitar,

 277

getting married, producing oodles of babies, landing my dream job as a fashion designer, breeding guinea pigs, making bread that doesn't taste like cardboard, scraping a pass in my maths GCSE, me reaching up to kiss Will, him bending down to touch his lips on the top of my head – the list was endless. I'd wanted all of these things before the accident but I longed for them even more now. I stared at the little gold stars painted on the ceiling above the altar.

"Reach for the stars, pet," Gramps used to say. "Dreams do come true."

I closed my eyes and remembered the heaviness of his arm around me as we shared a carol sheet the Christmas before he died. I heard the heart-breaking solo of 'Once in Royal David's City' bouncing off the pillars, smelled the tingly pine scent of the huge Norwegian spruce, felt the warmth of the candles flickering at the end of each pew. I would never know another Christmas, that magical time when this whole building seemed to vibrate with love, forgiveness and wonder.

Now, as I sat in a place where dreams are born and put to rest, I wondered what my funeral service would be like. It probably wouldn't be here unless the whole school attended. More likely it would take place at St Mary's because that's where I was christened. It isn't a particularly big church but I thought it would be spacious enough.

I'd only been to one funeral in my entire life and that was for Gramps. There were so many people there that loads of them had to stand at the back and around the sides. Mum and her brother had stood up and said lovely things about him. Some of what they said made people laugh, but not me. I just wept and wept until my breastbone felt bruised and my eyes were so puffed up that I could hardly see. Gran didn't cry at all, which I sort of admired but it shocked me too. She was as rigid and upright as the hard wooden pews that we squeezed onto. Her bright red lipstick was perfectly applied and she wore her black patent shoes. Gramps always loved her in those high heels and I hoped he was looking down at her, full of appreciation.

I wondered if there would be lots of tears at my funeral. It's bound to be different when you're

279

only fourteen. I hoped Mum and Dad wouldn't pick dreary hymns and I dreaded everyone wearing black – the more colour the better in my opinion.

Who would speak about me and my short life and what on earth would they find to say? Maybe Mrs Baxter would walk to the front and say something like 'Jessica has not yet achieved her potential' or 'Jessica doesn't make the most of her abilities' or 'Room for improvement'. That last one was definitely true. There's lots of room for improvement on being dead.

Disappointment swamped me. I didn't like any of those words for a parting shot, but what could I do about it now? I'd always held a little bit of myself back, felt the need to protect myself, felt I'd got plenty of time to release the real me. I cringed. What a waste. If I had another chance there was so much I could do, so much more I could be. I could be a better daughter, sister and friend to start with.

I curled my legs up underneath me and wondered what my friends would say once I'd gone for good. Maybe that I was generous, kind and loyal. But would they really believe it? Was it really true? I'd tried to be, but I didn't always succeed. Perhaps, temporarily numbed by a collective cloud of grief they'd manage to delude themselves for a time, forget my failings. Once someone has died, people often seem to put a gloss on their characters, conveniently airbrushing out all their faults. I lifted my head and stared at the altar.

"But I don't want my faults to be overlooked," I whispered. "I want time to put them right."

I listened in the silence for an answer, watched the motes of dust dance in the shaft of sunlight which poured through one of the top windows.

Dancing, parties – Gran and Gramps had loved a party. After Gramps's funeral we had gone back to the golf club where copious cups of tea had been served alongside the odd whisky. How anyone can eat at a funeral is beyond me but plenty of the previously distressed managed to stuff themselves with perfectly presented sandwiches and cajoling cakes. They talked about Gramps and laughed too loudly, as if they were at a party instead of a wake.

At the time it seemed wrong and I felt upset – I wanted to tell them to stop, to be quiet and sombre, but now I understood a bit better. Now I had changed my mind about what a wake should be. I wanted party food after my funeral, iced gems and pink wafer biscuits, cocktail sausages, teddy-bear-shaped crisps and bite-sized sandwiches with the crusts cut off. There had to be jelly, preferably orange-flavoured, with ice cream to accompany and bowls of hundreds and thousands to sprinkle over lavishly. Would Mum know how important it was that my funeral reflected the true me? I had no idea. It wasn't something we'd discussed over the cornflakes and I worried that she might be too distraught to care about the ceremonial side of things. When I went back home I would make a list and leave it somewhere obvious where Jamie would find it. I might not have been sure of my brother before the accident but I knew now that I could rely on him not to let me down.

Finally, I knelt down on the little tapestry hassock and prayed. I prayed for Mum and Dad, for Jamie, Gran and Sam, and for Kelly, Nat and Yas. I even prayed for Mrs Baxter and a few other teachers. I gave thanks for all the doctors and nurses who had looked after me in hospital and the man who had held my hand as I lay in the road after the accident. Eventually I said a little prayer for Will. I kept it as brief as possible, just a 'Dear God, please take care of Will'. I thought that it was more than he deserved. I didn't pray for Sara and it felt good to leave her out. Last of all, when everyone who mattered had been taken care of, I prayed for myself.

"Dear God," I murmured into the waiting stillness, "if there is any way this has been a horrible mistake, if there is any way out of this at all, please, please show me, before it is too late."

I paused, breathed in, sat very still.

"And if not, if it isn't a mistake, then please give me courage, help me to be brave and make my death as easy as possible for my family."

DESTINY

TUESDAY, 7 MARCH – 2.30 P.M.

I'd prayed loads of times before and never seemed to get an answer. Maths hadn't been wiped off the curriculum, Dad's mistress hadn't been struck down by a bolt of lightning, Gramps' cancer hadn't gone away. To be honest, I didn't really expect any response that time either.

I was crying when I left the church and my head was aching. As if to emphasise my fate, the church clock chimed two-thirty. I was into single figures now – only nine hours and thirty-one minutes to go.

Duke's Park was somewhere I always went to when I had a problem to sort out. There's a wildlife spinney where Gramps pointed out my first woodpecker, two tennis courts, a pitch and putt area which Will and Jamie use in the holidays and two play areas. At the far end is a limestone rockery which bursts with miniature daffodils and tulips in the spring. To one side of that is a brook with a little wooden bridge where we used to stand and play pooh sticks on our Sunday afternoon walks. A tarmac path loops around the whole area, and when I found out about Dad's affair I used to walk round and round the park. Somehow it helped to soothe me, to put things into some sort of perspective. I hoped it would have the same effect now.

Halfway round the park there was a strange smell. It was musty and sour. To begin with I thought it was the piles of damp leaves that had collected under the hedges, but it followed me into the open spaces, and when I settled on one of the bouncy horses in the pre-school play area it became even stronger. My nostrils felt as if they were swelling and I had the urge to sneeze. Normally, I felt safe in this little enclave with the trees sheltering the rear boundary and the happy memories floating around, but that smell made everything different. Then the roundabout began to spin, on its own. A hollow crater opened up in my chest ready to be filled with swirling panic.

The gentle rotation turned into a wild, energetic whirling. He wasn't to be seen, but he was there.

"Not again! Go away! This is beginning to feel like harassment."

I leapt from the horse and began to run but my legs felt as heavy as those buckets of wet sand that Jamie and I liked to mess around with when we were small. I fumbled with the catch on the gate. I could do it. I could get away from him if only I could get through that gate. Then I would be able to run and run and…

"Jessica! Wait!"

A heavenly handcuff clamped itself around my wrist and yanked me to a stop. You can't outwit an angel – not even one that doesn't look as if he enjoys exercise.

"That's right, you dislocate my shoulder as well," I snapped. "I've already hurt the other one jumping down from the school gate."

Darren had fully materialised now, all ruffled feathers and determined jawline.

"Goodness me, you're strong," he gasped.

He looked me up and down.

"Hasn't anyone ever told you it's rude to stare?"

I said, glaring back at him.

He shook his head and tut-tutted a few times.

"I was on my way back from dealing with another demise and I just couldn't get it out of my head, couldn't get *you* out of my head."

"I have that effect on people," I said, sulkily.

"You've been lying to me."

His eyes bored into mine.

"No I haven't. About what?"

"About looking different. It's the colours. I *knew* you were getting brighter, and I was right."

I looked down at myself. There was no hiding the fact. I glistened like a beautiful shoal of tropical fish just below the surface of the water.

"Oh, that." I snatched at an explanation. "I'm sure it's nothing to worry about. I mean, I couldn't have gone through all this and been the same, could I?"

He pursed his lips.

"I suppose not."

He glanced around the park. It was quiet, apart from a few people in the distance walking their dogs.

"All the same, I think we ought to be careful, maybe get you out of sight."

"It's fine," I said, trying to wriggle my wrist out of his grasp. "No one's spotted me yet."

"Are you sure?"

I hesitated. Once or twice I'd wondered if people were gazing in my direction or doing a double take as I walked past but I didn't want to let on to Darren.

"Of course."

"Hmm," he hummed, squinting as if he didn't really believe me. "And we want to keep it that way, don't we?"

His face invaded my personal space.

"I'm doing my best," I shot back. "It's not as if I can control what's happening to me. I'm not waving some magic wand and saying 'Hey Jess, let's bring on the bling and get brighter and brighter so that everyone can take a good look at you in your weird holographic form.'"

He arched backwards, loosening his grip slightly.

"Okay, point taken," he replied. "I'm sorry. I just can't afford to mess this up."

I noticed little beads of perspiration on his forehead and around his nose.

"Are you sweating?" I asked.

He wiped a hand across his face.

"It's all your fault. I've been in such a rush dealing with the dearly departed and having to keep a constant eye on you as well. It's more than any angel should be expected to cope with."

The musty, musky smell was much stronger.

"What *is* that smell?"

His cheeks flushed. He sniffed under his armpits.

"I think it's me," he said. "It's because I'm stressed. It'll soon pass."

"I hope so," I snapped. "It stinks."

"I'm sorry," he said.

So was I. I didn't mean to be unkind, even to him.

A dense black cloud blotted out the sun and it began to rain. Big, fat drops fell on us.

"Aargh!" he shrieked. "Moisture is very, very bad, and wet wings are the worst thing in this world and the next one. They weigh you down and take ages to dry."

I pointed to the play train in the corner.

"It's only a shower. Why don't you sit in there until it passes?"

His grip on my wrist tightened again.

"Only if you come too. You will come with me, won't you?"

"I haven't exactly got much choice," I said.

I helped to prise his precious wings into the little train and sat down opposite him. We didn't speak for ages, but just sat in an uncomfortable silence while I pushed a discarded sweet wrapper around with my foot.

"I don't like doing this, you know."

The softness in his voice caught me off guard.

"You could have fooled me."

He was quiet again.

"Things aren't always as they seem, Jessica."

I didn't trust this sudden change of mood. It was a trick. He leaned towards me.

"You of all people should know that."

"What do you mean?"

"Well, visiting your friends wasn't quite what you expected, was it? You found out a few secrets, didn't you, and had to face up to a few things?"

I didn't reply for a while, didn't want to be sucked into his web.

"This was meant to be *my* time with my friends. I thought it was going to be private," I said finally, with a glare. "You've been watching me every step of the way. It's not nice to spy on people."

"And *I* thought you'd follow my instructions," he replied. "I didn't intend for you to use the time to think about…" He lowered his voice. "… living."

He sighed. It was a brooding breath and a layer of frost coated the inside edges of the train.

"I've got a target to reach and I'm already behind. Only yesterday an elderly lady managed to dodge the death penalty so I probably won't get enough points to reach my end-of-the-week target."

"Good for her," I said.

He leaned forwards and covered his face with his hands.

"It's not fair. I'm trying so hard and all people want to do is drop out of dying."

"You can hardly blame them, can you?" I murmured. "I mean, if you'd had the choice, you wouldn't have opted to enter the Pearly Gates before you were ready, would you?"

He looked at me through his fingers and blinked several times. Slowly, he shook his head. There was a clatter as his halo fell to the floor. He left it there.

"I shouldn't be agreeing with you," he groaned. "Angels of death don't have doubts about what they're doing."

"And you do?" I asked.

"Sometimes," he murmured.

"Have you ever wondered if you're in the wrong job? Perhaps you should be doing something else – playing a harp or designing non-slip halos."

I picked his halo up off the floor, brushed it down and handed it back to him.

He almost smiled.

"There have been angels of death in my family for generations. I can't be the one to break the chain." He screwed up his face. "Destiny, eh?"

"It sucks, doesn't it?" I said.

"It sure does," he replied.

It seemed to break the ice. He relaxed, the frost melted and that cloying, sickly scent went away.

We sat together like friends, and while the rain clattered on to the roof of the play train I told him everything I'd learned over the last few days.

I talked about Nat and how I'd known that she'd got a problem with food but hadn't wanted to face up to it. I told him how guilty I felt about not helping Kelly more when her mum left and how pleased and surprised I was that she and Jamie had got together. I told him that I'd always thought Yasmin was really clever, and although I'd known that she worked hard, I'd never realised how much pressure she was under from her parents. I told him about Will and Sara and how hurt and betrayed I felt. He was a good listener. He listened with his whole body, not just his delicate, angelic ears. I told him about all the things that I still wanted to achieve and I railed at the unfairness of it all.

"I've learned such a lot in the last few days," I said. "I've learned how to be a better person and what's the point if I can't put any of it into practice?"

His gaze was soft, sympathetic.

"You've got a good point, Jessica Rowley," he said.

293

He spun his halo on one finger. I watched as it glinted in a pale ray of sunlight which peeped out from behind a cloud.

"We might be able to see a rainbow," I said, sticking my head outside and tasting droplets of rain on my tongue. He poked his head out of the window next to mine and we both looked up at the sky.

"I like you, Jessica Rowley," he said. "I didn't expect to meet a client quite like you."

"Well, get used to it," I said. "I'm a lightweight in the determination stakes compared to other people. You'd better toughen up or you'll be totally stressed out trying to get the really obstinate ones over to the other side."

"Really?" he asked.

"Definitely," I added. "Didn't *you* put up a fight?"

"No chance," he replied. "Car accident. There one minute, gone the next."

"I'm sorry," I replied. "But if you had lingered a bit, you'd have wanted to cling on to this world, wouldn't you, especially if you were only fourteen and had barely started living?"

"Yes, I suppose I would."

"There!" I said, pointing to where the rainbow arc rose above the trees. "Isn't it beautiful?"

I looked at him. "I always used to think that rainbows were a sign that something good was going to happen."

"Me too," he replied.

I couldn't be sure whether it was a raindrop or a tear clinging to his lower lashes.

"And you're one hundred per cent sure that there isn't a way out of this?" I asked.

When I asked that question I never thought about the price I might have to pay. Instead, I thought only of myself.

Gran's frowning face floated before my eyes. "Be careful what you wish for, Jess."

I ignored the warning and opened my eyes pleadingly wide. He shook his head in exasperation.

"You don't give up, do you, Jessica Rowley?"

I grinned.

"No, I don't, do I? At least not until I absolutely have to."

He stared up at the rainbow.

"If I got found out…"

He drew a finger across his throat.

A surge of energy engulfed me.

"You won't," I whispered. "I promise. Tell me what it is and I'll do it. Anything."

"You won't like it."

He wouldn't look me in the eye. I should have backed off there and then.

"I don't like Brussels sprouts," I said, "but I'll eat them if my life depends upon it."

He wavered. I grabbed his smooth, cold hand.

"At least give me the choice," I begged. "Surely that's not too much to ask?"

So he told me of the alternative. I should have listened to Gran's words. Sometimes it really is better not to wish at all.

ALTERNATIVES

TUESDAY, 7 MARCH – 3.50 P.M.

"Someone else could take your place."

I pulled my head back inside the play train.

"That's fantastic!"

Immediately I felt guilty. Where was my sense of decency?

"Nothing worth having comes easily." I heard Gran's warning voice inside my head. Unease latched on to me like those ticks that Will's dog gets when he goes into the fields in summertime. I tried to ignore it, and leaned forward to shake Darren's hand. We had a pact. Better not to think about the details. He shrank away, not mirroring my smile.

"Don't you want to know who?"

"No. No, I don't."

It was mercenary of me but, if it was someone I didn't know, I could cope.

"I think you should."

Time seemed to be suspended, prising the words out of me.

"N-not one of my family? Not Gran?"

He shook his head. I closed my eyes gratefully and let my head flop forwards. The relief was short-lived.

"It can't be anyone random."

My lids flipped up. I was to be wrenched out of my cowardice after all.

"It's got to be someone of a similar age, the same sex," he continued.

I bit my lip.

"But it will be a stranger?"

I knew the answer before I asked the question.

"It's not that simple," he said softly.

"Who then?"

He coughed and placed his halo neatly around his knees.

"It has to be someone who's almost the same height as you, similar in looks, someone I can pass off as your double when the celestial light is shining in St Peter's eyes."

It was obvious who he meant but at least he was trying to let me down lightly. I was grateful.

"You mean Sara, don't you?"

He blinked, and looked down at his bare feet with their buffed toe nails while I let the information sink in. Option 1 – I could kill Sara. Option 2 – I leave things as they are.

"It's got to be her," he said. "I'm sorry."

He sounded as if he meant it.

"But she's my best friend."

He raised a perfectly plucked eyebrow.

"Don't you mean *was* your best friend? Besides, you did wish she was dead only yesterday evening."

"I didn't mean it, and you know I didn't."

He shrugged. My heart was cracking like the glaze on one of Gran's Chinese eggshell ornaments.

"I can't do it."

"Despite what she's done to you?"

Hot tears began to trickle down my cheeks. Doubt was already wheedling its way through me. It was all so unfair. I thought of Sara and Will together, now and in the future. It hurt so much. But did I really hate her enough to do *that*?

"There must be another way."

I wished I could have sounded more assertive

but his offer was too tempting. I'd be an idiot to turn it down.

Darren touched my arm.

"There isn't. It's late to be making a substitution. I haven't got time to find anyone else."

I blinked at him. Still I held back.

"You can't expect me to decide here, now. I need time to think."

He tapped his silver watch and spoke oh, so softly.

"It's my turn to remind you, Jessica, that there isn't much time."

"When do you need to know?" I asked.

He placed his halo back on his head and half stood up.

"I'll give you as long as I can."

He was quiet for a moment and I could almost see the calculations going on inside his head.

"I tell you what – why don't we meet in the hospital car park at seven-thirty, so you can let me know what you've decided? I do need a few hours if I've got to make alternative arrangements."

He was in business mode again. He made the whole situation sound so matter-of-fact, as if I was just swapping places with someone for a game of hockey. Except this was the game of Life and Death and it was Sara or me. My resolve to be a good and decent person was in bits. In my mind Sara deserved to pay for what she had done but this was the ultimate price. Could I really go through with it?

Darren stepped out of the play train and unfurled his wings, flapping them a couple of times. I clutched at his sleeve.

"I don't know what to do."

I hated myself for even saying that, for even considering condemning my best friend to death. How could I be so callous? He looked down at my fingers. I thought he was going to pluck them away but he covered them with his hand.

"No," he replied. "It's a tough one."

"If I decided to save myself…" I hesitated, almost choking on the words. "W-what would happen to Sara? How would she die?"

"I can't tell you that."

"Why not?"

He sighed, coating my face with coolness.

"It's confidential information, Jessica. I can't

 301

tell you everything. I'm already breaking the rules for you and risking my job."

He braced his wings, ready for flight. I wanted to delay him, to put off the moment when my thoughts wouldn't have anyone else to contain them.

"Can we meet inside?" I begged. "By the chocolate machine? It'll be dark and cold in the car park."

His eyes became wary.

"I don't like hospitals much."

I was sure he shrank a little, looked smaller, vulnerable, like someone trapped in an afterlife they don't want to live.

"I don't like dying much."

He looked taken aback by the anger in my voice, or maybe it was the heat radiating from my cheeks. He looked straight into my eyes.

"Then don't do it. You know you don't want to."

As if he knew that he'd said too much, he powered down the path and soared up above the trees towards the rainbow. I watched him as the current of air turned the sky to watermarked silk around him, and then he was gone, leaving just a fading ripple behind. I was alone.

CHOOSING

TUESDAY, 7 MARCH – 5.00 P.M.

I walked. Steam rose from the tarmac as the sun warmed it. Someone was mowing the grass, weaving in and out of the trees. A dog waddled up and sniffed my hand. I'd always wanted a dog. How could I bear to leave all of this behind? But could I live with myself for the next sixty or seventy years if I sacrificed Sara? That was basically murder, wasn't it? However much she had hurt me, wouldn't I be hurting myself even more if I killed her off? It was an impossible decision, the sort that you could mull over for a million years and not resolve. Except I didn't have that long. I didn't even have a million seconds. The only thing I could think of to do was to go home and draw up a list. Maybe then I would know what to do.

Life v Death

1. I kill Sara
   a) I LIVE
   b) Mum and Dad's lives aren't ruined.
   c) Dad might give up his other woman and come back to us.
   d) Jamie might just pull himself around and not flunk his exams which will ruin the rest of his life.
   e) Sam will get her doting mistress back.
   f) I get the chance to be a better friend to everyone in the whole world.
   g) Will is so overcome with guilt at allowing himself to have been hooked by Sara that he'll fall at my feet in a display of undying love and be unable to refuse anything I ask of him for the rest of our lives.
   h) That last one means that I get the ultimate revenge on Sara for stealing Will.

I paused and chewed the end of my pen. Frankly it sounded like a no-brainer, and there were millions more points that I could have added, but those seemed to be the most important ones and I was a bit short of time. So I decided to move on to the next bit.

2. I leave things as they are
   a) I DIE
   b) The future of everyone I love is altered forever and ever and not in a good way.
   c) The trauma of my death might lead to Mum and Dad splitting up or it could work the other way around and bring them back together.

(That's the trouble with lists: there's always one bit that doesn't totally fit into one category.)

   d) If I die and Mum and Dad fall apart, Gran might have to do

305

even more than she's doing now.
How would she cope with that?
Would it make her ill?

e) Would Yasmin forever blame herself
for not making me walk all the way
home on the night of the accident?

f) Would Nat starve herself to death
or torture her body until it was
so damaged that she couldn't have
children?

g) Maybe Kelly would step in and hold
everyone together but she'd be so
exhausted that she'd have to give
up her sport.

Then there was Sara. I wrote slowly, forming the letters with care.

h) SARA LIVES

I stared at those two little words, trying to work out what I was feeling. It was such a strange mixture. I might have hated her, but in a strange way I still loved her too. You can't just cut ties with people, like snipping through a ribbon, not if you've known them for most of your life. They are part of you, and however much you wish it wasn't true they will always be a part of your past, helping to make you who you are. If I died she might get her hands on Will, but would it last? Would she eventually regret what she'd done? And what about his friendship with Jamie? I couldn't believe my brother would condone what was going on.

I suddenly realised how the consequences of my death would ripple outwards beyond even the realms of my over-active imagination. Part of me still couldn't believe that it was really going to happen. I loved my imperfect, muddled lottery of a life and more than anything I wanted to carry on living it.

"We don't always get what we want, Jess."

Those were Gran's words after Gramps had died. I had sat on her sofa and sobbed as she held me close.

"I didn't want him to die," I'd cried. "Why did he have to die?"

 307

"We all have to go sometime, sweetheart," she had said. "It was his time."

And now it was mine. But I was only fourteen and Gramps had been seventy-two. He'd had fifty-eight more years than I was going to get and he still wasn't ready to go. He'd fought and fought to stay with us. It wasn't fair. None of it was fair. I was shaking as I screwed up my list and threw it in the bin.

The bracket clock in the hall chimed five and I went through to Jamie's room. He stayed late at school on a Tuesday but I knew that within the next few minutes, if the bus was on time, I would hear his key jiggle in the lock. I tucked my funeral instructions between the pages of his *Complete Who's Who of Test Cricketers*. It was the page with Kevin Pieterson on, and Jamie fancied himself as a bit of a demon batsman so that section was well thumbed. I'd written the note in pink ink and I left a corner peeking out of the top of the book just to be sure he didn't miss it.

Sure enough, I'd barely wandered back onto the landing when I saw him loping up the path. I went downstairs and waited while he dropped his bag inside the front door and slung his jacket over the banisters. In the kitchen I leaned against the radiator and revelled in the warmth permeating my legs. The kettle was boiling on the hob, and out of the window I could see Gran tidying up the herbaceous border. Jamie poked his head out of the back door.

"You here again, Gran?"

She looked up and waved.

"Like a bad penny, me," she replied. "Kettle's on. Do you want a cup of tea?"

"I'll make it," Jamie replied. "Where's Mum?"

"At the hospital. She's feeling better."

I saw Jamie's startled look and Gran's immediate recognition of what she'd said.

"Your mum, I meant. Her migraine's gone."

"Oh!"

His disappointment flooded the kitchen. As he poured boiling water into the teapot, his mobile rang.

"Hi!" he said. "You okay?"

I could tell that he was talking to Kelly from the way his features had softened. He stirred the tea around in the pot and put the lid in place.

"Yeah, I've spoken to him. In fact, it wasn't difficult after all because Will mentioned it to *me*."

Jamie moved to the window and stared out. I looked at his back, the way his white shirt suddenly looked too small. It was tight across the shoulders and the seam was coming apart just under the arm.

"He seems quite cut up about it. It's almost as if he feels that he's let Jess down."

Yep, I thought. If Will's talking about his relationship with Sara, he's absolutely right. I moved closer to try to hear what Kelly was saying but she kept her voice low so I had to be content with Jamie's part of the conversation.

"Apparently Sara contacted *him*. He doesn't know how she got his number. He thought it might be from me – anyway, it wasn't. She suggested they met up in town, said she was feeling really upset about Jess and wanted to talk to someone about it."

Jamie nodded as Kelly obviously made some rude remark at the end of the phone.

"Yes, I know. He feels a bit stupid now but he had no idea that she fancied him. Why would he? He thought he was just doing her a favour, doing Jess a favour."

Oh, how my heart swelled at those words!

"Apparently she kissed him."

"WHAT?"

I did hear that. Kelly shouted so loudly that Jamie jerked the phone away from his ear.

"Actually, Will says that he feels a bit sorry for her. He thinks she's not handling it at all well and she just wants some comfort."

"Yeah, right!" Kelly's sarcasm was like a fist banging down on the table.

I knew what she'd probably be thinking as well – that Sara should be turning to her friends for comfort, to Nat and Yasmin and to Kelly herself.

"He's not going to see her again, though," Jamie continued.

He ran a finger around the inside of his collar.

"You know what? Secretly I think he quite likes Jess."

I almost staggered and knocked into the table. Really? Will liked me? Why on earth hadn't he said? I couldn't believe it. How unfair was that? Jamie moved to the cupboard and took out two mugs.

"I've got to go, Kel. Mum's with Jess so my

gran's here. She doesn't like me coming back to an empty house. I'm making her some tea. Speak later?"

I left him opening a bottle of milk and wandered back through my home, trying to take in the information about Will, trying to take in all sorts of other things that I had barely noticed when I lived there: the variety of Mum's gardening books, the scorch mark on the rug in front of the fireplace, the intricate detail of the cornice in the sitting room. I even went into the garage and trailed my fingers over Jamie's muddy golf clubs before clasping Dad's latest seed packets to my heart. Surely he couldn't be intending to leave us if he was planning to plant lettuce and radish? On a shelf in the conservatory some sweet peas were sprouting. They're another of my favourite flowers. The label read 'Little Sweetheart' in Dad's untidy handwriting.

"Oh Dad," I said. "I'm sorry I was so mean to you. It wasn't right what you did to us, but I never stopped loving you."

I'd thought about visiting his other woman but part of me hadn't wanted to. Besides, I hadn't had enough time and it was probably a good thing not to. If she'd been young, stunning and not much older than me it would have been awful, but if she'd been old and ugly that would have been even worse. Gran's right – some things are better left undisturbed.

In the garden, tadpoles wiggled in the pond and forget-me-nots frothed on the rockery. Every blade of grass, every twig and flower, every clump of soil seemed to imprint its memory into my soul. I was in physical pain now. My whole body ached from sadness.

While I'd been out someone, presumably Dad, had taken my trampoline out of its winter hibernation and set it up in the middle of the lawn. I wondered why. Did he know something I didn't, or was it just a symbol of hope? I climbed on to it and bounced lightly, expecting to feel weak, fragile enough to be swept away by the slightest breeze, but the springs creaked and I could see Gran, sipping her tea in the kitchen, peering out of the window. I climbed down, half-wishing that I could bounce up into the sky and be whisked away there and then, away from the people and places

I loved so much, without a backwards glance. In some ways that would make everything easier. At least I wouldn't have to make the nightmare of a decision about who was going to die, Sara or me.

Samantha was busy munching grass in her outside run. When Jamie had gone upstairs and Gran was busy peeling vegetables at the sink, I lifted her out. She snuggled up close, her tiny heart beating against where mine should be, and I buried my nose in her fur. She squeaked twice.

"I love you, Sammie," I whispered. "You're the best guinea pig in the whole world. I've got to go now. I can't say for how long because I don't know what I'm going to do. If I don't come back, Sammie, you mustn't worry. Jamie will look after you. Be a good girl for him. No nipping."

I put her back in the run and she pressed her nose up against the wire. It was as if she knew that we might not see each other again.

I stepped inside the kitchen and looked at Gran rinsing the potatoes in cold water.

"Thank you for everything, Gran," I whispered. "Thank you for loving me so much, for always being there for me when I needed you, for teaching me about plants and birds and trees and history. It was special, every bit of it. You're special. I want us to have more happy times together. I don't know what to do, Gran. I wish I could ask you for some advice."

I blew her the softest of kisses and tiptoed across the floor behind her. As I went past, she turned around and brushed a bit of her fine whitish hair back behind her ear. She stood very still, saucepan in one hand, only her eyes moving around the room. I knew she had sensed my presence and I was glad. It meant that we still had a special bond.

On the landing I stood outside Jamie's bedroom door and spread my fingers against the white paintwork.

"I've come to say goodbye, Jamie, just in case. I'm not sure yet what's going to happen. One minute I think one thing and the next I've changed my mind. I want to be noble but Darren's offer really is too good to refuse, don't you think? I'd be stupid to turn it down and waste everything that I've learned in the last few days, wouldn't I?

315

Anyway, if I do turn all heroic and end up sacrificing myself I want you to take care of yourself. Take care of Kelly and Will and Mum and Dad too. Don't forget Sam either. Whether I'm here or not I want you to have a good life, Jamie. Don't waste a single second of it. If I don't come back you must live your life for both of us."

There was a lump in my throat now and I could hardly speak the words. In my bedroom I changed back into the hospital gown and sat on the end of my bed, praying for a miracle so I wouldn't have to make this choice. I knew it was impossible. Miracles didn't happen to ordinary people like me.

HONOUR

TUESDAY, 7 MARCH – 7.38 P.M.

I never did work well to deadlines and I was late. Darren was already waiting in the hospital foyer, standing next to the chocolate machine just as I'd asked. I'd half expected him to be outside. After all, he had the upper hand in this relationship. It seemed like the smallest of concessions but it made me feel as if I mattered to him, at least a little bit. He was pressed against the wall as if trying to imprint his wings onto the sage green paint. He looked like one of those butterflies pinned into glass cases, except for the fact he was trembling all over. Even the highlighted tips of his hair were shivering.

"What's the matter?"

No answer. He just chewed on his bottom lip so hard he could have drawn blood if he'd

317

had any. His eyes flickered around like a lizard's when it's searching for its next meal. They were looking at everything except at me. His face was pale and drawn and his halo was tilted. My heart lurched. Had he already killed off Sara in a burst of angelic enthusiasm? Was that why I felt so strong on the trampoline? Was that why my yellow ballet pumps had made imprints in the damp grass verge as I made my way to the hospital? Was that why I felt colder than I ever had in my entire life? Were all of these signs that Sara was dead and I had been spared? If that was the case I should have felt elated, shouldn't I? But I didn't. I just felt sick.

A middle-aged couple plodded past. I rubbed my hands together, trying to warm myself up, and moved closer to Darren. We were almost touching.

"What have you done with Sara?"

I almost choked on the words.

He looked down at me.

"Nothing… yet."

Oh, the relief. It was so unexpected and I hugged myself. I could have hugged him. The tears flowed again.

"Don't cry, Jessica," I told myself sternly. Where

was Mrs Baxter when I needed her? I could hear her voice now: "There's no point working yourself up into a state. That's not going to solve anything, now is it, Jessica dear?"

More people wandered past, clutching bags of fresh nightwear, magazines, sweets, all of those things that make a hospital stay more bearable. Nobody glanced in our direction but I felt conspicuous, as if I was about to be spotted and told off for being in the wrong place, as if some bossy nurse would come over and say, "What are you doing down here, Jessica Rowley? Upstairs to bed with you right now. You can't die in the foyer. That would be very inconvenient."

"We can't talk here," I sniffed. "There are a couple of small rooms near to mine. The staff use them for private conversations with patients' relatives. I know because one of the doctors took Mum and Dad in there soon after I arrived."

I went to take his hand.

"Come with me."

He grabbed hold of the chocolate machine with such force that everything inside it shook.

319

The foyer was a carbon copy of a waxwork museum as people stopped and stared. Could everyone see us now? Could they see me with my soft blue and yellow jewel colours shimmering like one of Gran's floaty scarfs? Could they fathom out the rainbow cusp between life and death?

"What *is* the matter?" I whispered to him.

"I can't go through there." He nodded his head towards the swing doors which led into the main body of the building.

"Why not? Have you been banned?"

Chocolate bars began to make suicidal leaps into the tray at the bottom of the machine. I grabbed his clammy hand.

"For goodness' sake, get a grip of yourself. You're the one who's meant to be an oasis of tranquillity here and I'm the one in turmoil. Come on, we're attracting attention."

"And whose fault is that?" he moaned. "Look at you! You're so bright, so strong. You could almost be human."

"But I'm not, am I? And neither are you. One of those people peering in our direction may have psychic powers for all we know. In next to no time we'll have a load of reporters and ghostbusters on our trail."

He let out a little wail and I managed to pull him towards the stairs, thanking my lucky stars that he hadn't been bingeing on ambrosia or whatever it is that heavenly hosts indulge in. Despite the fact he wasn't heavy, he still left belligerent scuff marks on the carpet, little fluorescent trails that would have the world intrigued for months if not years to come.

By the time I'd hauled him upstairs and along the corridor he was just about hysterical. I pushed him into the tiny room and shut the door behind us. There was a frosted window with some fake flowers on the sill, a couple of comfortable chairs and a table with a box of tissues in the centre. The whole place reeked of grief. I knew in an instant that this was where they took people to give them bad news. Perhaps that's why the room was so small, to contain all that emotion, stop it spilling out and magnifying too soon, too publicly.

I was about to tell him to sit down when he dived head first into one of the armchairs, curled up his legs underneath him like a wounded child and completely covered himself with his wings.

Momentarily, I felt sorry for him. We were both out of place in this world but his behaviour was not what I needed. Surely he realised that I had enough problems without having to deal with a distraught angel?

"What is it with you and hospitals?" I asked, trying to keep my tone as understanding as possible.

"They make me feel ill," he mumbled.

"Yeah, me too."

I couldn't control the sarcasm.

He lifted one wing so that I could see his chin and trembling lower lip.

"It's since my mum died," he said in a small, childlike voice. "It brings it all back."

I sat down next to him and stroked the silver-tipped feathers at the edge of one wing.

"I'm sorry. How old were you?"

"Six. It was cancer."

"My gramps had cancer too."

He moved his head to one side so I could just see half of his face.

"My grandfather died when I was a baby and I never knew my dad. After Mum died it was just Gran and me." He paused. "She's all on her own now."

"She must miss you."

He nodded.

"I miss her too."

He twisted more in the chair. His cheeks were tear-stained. I passed him a tissue.

"Perhaps you can take a break, apply for some holiday and pay her a visit," I suggested.

He blew his nose very loudly.

"I wish. There's barely any time off in this job."

"And I've taken up loads of your time because I've been so difficult," I said. "I'm really sorry."

"It's all right," he said, dropping the tissue in the bin. "I haven't minded that much."

Some colour was beginning to come back into his cheeks and he had stopped quivering.

In the distance a tea trolley rumbled down the corridor. I needed to get this over with, to say it out loud, to commit myself.

"I didn't want to tell you of my decision in

the car park, in the dark. It seemed too impersonal."

He sat very still.

"I already know what it is," he said.

"Really?" I felt slightly annoyed. "I'm not sure how. I didn't know myself until a few minutes ago." If you knew what I was going to say, why did we have to meet up?" I asked. "Why have you put yourself and me through all of this stress?"

He looked at me, blinking fast.

"I needed to see you, to look into your eyes, to know that you mean it."

I moved my face closer to his, opened my eyes wide.

"And do I?"

He nodded.

"Yes, I'm afraid you do, Jessica. No substitution. I don't suppose it was ever in much doubt, was it? You're too nice a person to do something like that."

"I don't feel very nice. I did consider it. I'd almost convinced myself that she ought to take my place. But that was wrong. However mean she's been, she doesn't deserve that."

Suddenly, he looked cross.

"I'll tell you what she doesn't deserve," he said, "a friend like you. After all, she betrayed you big time with that boy."

"His name's Will," I said, "and I do appreciate the offer to swap, but how could I go forward and make a good life for myself if I'd bumped off my best friend? You do understand, don't you?"

He shrugged.

"I suppose you've got a point."

"Revenge isn't the answer," I said. "It would prevent me from being the sort of person I wanted to be."

The lights hummed; the air was heady and clinging.

"I thought you'd be pleased. I must have saved you quite a lot of bother."

"I should be pleased, shouldn't I?"

He looked down at the carpet tiles, studying a stain where someone had spilled some coffee.

"Are all angels as difficult as you?" I put a smile in my voice.

"Probably not." He shrugged. "I don't know. We work independently most of the time."

What was the matter with him? Had he really wanted me to swap places with Sara?

"Cheer up," I said. "You might get promoted soon – probably a nice new outfit with an extra-blingy halo to match, and maybe even a harp. You *can* say thanks."

"Thanks."

It seemed to be all I was going to get. I stood up, wondering what to do next. Should I just go back to my bed? I didn't know the procedure for this sort of thing.

"It's no good." His face scrunched up like an uncared-for piece of linen. "I don't think I can do it. I like you, Jessica," he said, quietly. "I admire you: you're a real fighter, and you're honourable. You deserve another chance."

"WHAT? You told me that I couldn't have another chance, that you didn't have control over life and death!"

"I don't."

I stared at him, open-mouthed, the reality of what he was saying sinking in.

"Then the only way out of this is for you to take Sara," I said, "and I absolutely forbid that."

He cracked his knuckles, cowered in the chair.

"Don't shout at me," he whinged. "I can't bear people shouting."

"You have to promise that you won't take Sara instead of me."

"All right," he sighed. "I promise."

Was he telling the truth? I couldn't be sure but I thought so.

"I'm sorry that I shouted," I lowered my voice, "but this decision to die is the hardest I've ever had to make. I wanted someone to tell me I was doing the right thing."

I hesitated, stuttered.

"I w-wanted you to be proud of me."

He wouldn't meet my gaze. The sentence seemed to take on a form like those banners that trail behind planes. It hung between us.

"I am proud of you."

It was the softest of whispers. He stood up and folded me in his wings, resting his head on mine.

"I'm really, really proud of you," he murmured. "If I was in your position I wouldn't have behaved nearly as well."

We stayed like that for ages, neither of us able to break apart.

"Is this what it will be like?" I asked. "When it's time to go, will I feel like this? Will I feel safe and cherished?"

"Yes," he whispered. "Of course you will. You *are* cherished, Jessica Rowley, by more people than you'll ever realise."

"Then it'll be all right," I said, and I rested my face against his chest.

It was the nurse with the tea trolley who broke us up, bustling in and collecting an empty cup as we clung to each other, the executioner and his victim, minutes away from the point of no return. I was the one to take a step back. He didn't let go but wiped away my tears with his feathers.

"I'd better be going then," I said, "back to my bed – to wait."

He nodded. He was crying too.

"You're in the wrong job." I smiled. "You should be a guardian angel. You'd be a natural at that. You're good at keeping tabs on people."

He returned my smile and I pulled away.

"I'm going now. Either Mum or Dad will be by my bed and I want to spend a bit of time with them before... Thanks for everything. I know not many people get the chance of a few extra days or to visit their friends like I have. It was great.

"Just one last question. Will I ever be able to come back again and see how everyone's getting on?"

Big angelic tears fell from his eyes but I stayed calm.

"Maybe," he gulped, "if they really need you."

"Well, that's not so bad then, is it?" I sighed. "And would they know that I was there?"

He held out his hands, palms upturned.

"I hope so. I can't answer that. Maybe, sometimes, some of them would."

I swallowed, nodded, and placed my hands on top of his.

"I guess I'll see you later then. It will be you waiting for me, won't it?"

"Of course it will be me. I wouldn't entrust you to anyone else."

He lifted my hand to his lips and kissed it.

 329

His lips were like a splash of sparkling water.

"It's been a pleasure to meet you, Jessica Rowley."

"I don't think you mean that."

"Oh, but I do. I really do."

I smiled and drew away.

"We may not have hit it off to start with and the circumstances aren't exactly ideal but actually it's been a pleasure to meet you too."

It was time to go.

"Will you be all right getting out of here? Do you want me to take you downstairs?"

"No, I'll be okay. Thanks for the offer, though."

I touched his arm.

"Darren, don't forget what I said about your gran. Try to take some time off. Go and see her. It would do you both good."

He blinked several times.

"You're very wise for one so young, Jessica Rowley."

"No one's ever called me wise before. Thank you. It's a nice word to end with."

And I turned my back on him and left to prepare for my death.

WILL

TUESDAY, 7 MARCH – 8.42 P.M.

"So this is it," I said to myself in the mirror of the ladies' toilets. I smoothed my hair and ran a finger over my eyebrows to give them a lift before taking off the ballet pumps and leaving them neatly under one of the sinks. I felt incredibly calm as I walked down the corridor, the floor cold and smooth against my bare feet.

A nurse was coming out of the room and I caught the door before she managed to close it behind her. We had a bit of a tug of war. She checked along the bottom to see why it had momentarily jammed and I slipped through.

I hadn't bothered to peek in at the little window to see who was involved in the evening vigil because I knew it wasn't Gran or Jamie. I'd left them at home so it was bound to be Mum and maybe Dad too, if I was lucky. I wanted them both to be there. Of course, if my medical state had suddenly deteriorated it could have been all four of them. Gran and Jamie could easily have driven to the hospital in half the time it took me to make my way back there.

My brother *was* perched on the window sill and again I felt that pulsating where my heart should be. I was obviously a lot worse. As I dared to look at my shell, there was someone else sitting next to my body and it was someone I wouldn't have expected to see there in a million years. It was Will. In one hand he held a small brown teddy bear. It had a white satin heart stitched to its tummy embroidered with the words 'Get Well Soon' and, as he leaned forwards, Will's other hand was almost touching mine.

I just stood in the middle of the room, feeling as if I was taking part in the best dream and worst nightmare, all rolled into one. He looked absolutely amazing. His hair was all tousled and he was wearing blue jeans with a rip at the knee and a black and white checked shirt.

Why was he here? Why now? I should have felt dizzy with happiness but suddenly I felt really weary and leaned back against the wall to steady myself. Where was Mum? Did she know that Will was here? How could Jamie do this to me? I couldn't bear Will's last memory of me to be so gruesome. I forced my eyes away from his concerned face and studied my shell, prepared for the worst. I was surprised. There was a definite improvement. My skin looked smoother, my eyelashes had lost that desiccated look and my lips were properly pink. Despite that, I still looked as bland as a blancmange. It was as if someone had stolen my essence. I didn't look like the sort of person you remember for your entire life, and I did want Will to think about me from time to time.

I wondered how long he'd been sitting by my bed and could have kicked myself for not getting there earlier. I pressed my forehead in frustration and my elbow knocked against the light switch.

"How did that happen?" Will gasped as the lights went off and then on again.

Jamie's eyes widened and he lifted his hands up in the air.

"Weird things have been happening all week,"

he said. "I've been going into Jess's bedroom every day to feed Sam and things have been changing places."

"That'll be your mum or your gran," Will replied.

His fingers were almost touching mine, edging closer, a centimetre at a time. Was he doing that unconsciously or didn't he want Jamie to notice?

"I don't think so. Dad won't let anyone move a thing. He says everything must be left just as it is for when Jess comes home. Gran doesn't go in there much. She finds it too upsetting, and Mum just sits on the bed and stares into space. It's as if..."

"What?" Will prompted.

Jamie laughed nervously.

"Promise you won't laugh?"

"Of course not," Will replied.

"It's as if Jess has been there, in her room. It's not just the things moving. I can sort of feel her presence."

I made a little whistling sound with my breath – my brother, the intuitive one. That was another surprise. Jamie gestured towards the bed.

"It's weird, isn't it? She looks like Jess but at the same time there's something missing."

They both stared at my body as if they were trying to look through my outer covering and into my core. Will's fingers stroked the sheet. Our skin was a millimetre apart now. If I could just stretch out… maybe it would be like the magic kiss in fairy tales. Maybe Will could save me. Even at this stage, that bit of hope was stuck to my aura like the most stubborn of sticky labels.

"She was here," Jamie interrupted my day-dream, "until a few days ago. Then, one afternoon I turned up and something was different. It was as if – as if she'd already gone."

His voice trailed away. They sat in silence until it was broken by my brother's sobs. I'd never heard him cry like that before.

"Why does it take losing someone to make you realise how much they mean to you?" he choked. "Why couldn't I admit to her how special she is? Why couldn't I just show her how much I loved her instead of arguing with her all of the time?"

"It's not just you, Jamie," I cried from deep inside. "It was me too. I could have said those things to you."

"She knows, Jamie," Will said. "If she could talk she'd be saying exactly the same thing to you too."

Wow! How spooky was that?

"You really think so?" Jamie gulped.

Will dragged his fingers through his hair and looked down at me tenderly.

"Yes, I do," he said, and I loved him in that moment, truly loved him. It wasn't some adolescent crush. It was a lasting love, a love that would endure whatever he did because I knew that he understood me and that he could never, ever deliberately hurt me.

Will got up and went to pat Jamie on the shoulder. My brother dragged his sleeve across his eyes and I took the opportunity to slip back into my body. It wasn't as easy as I'd expected. It was as if I'd become too big for my shell, like folding up a sleeping bag and squeezing it back into its sack. I wondered if I'd burst at the seams.

"I've got to go," Will said. "I'm really sorry."

"It's okay. I'm okay. Not meeting someone, are you?" There was a teasing but anxious note in Jamie's voice. I tensed.

"Don't worry. I won't fall for that one again –

not that she'll try it. I made it quite clear that I wasn't interested, not in the way she was hoping for anyway."

My heart felt as if it was soaring away towards the ceiling. How could I feel so happy and so sad at the same time?

"I've got to practise my guitar for a lesson tomorrow. That's a lot safer," Will said.

"No strings attached," Jamie joked.

Will and I groaned together. That was more like the Jamie we knew and tolerated.

"Can I visit again?" Will asked. I sensed him move back to my side.

"If you like." Jamie was *so* unenthusiastic, I could have hit him. Of course Will could visit, every day if he wanted to – except that there wouldn't be any more days.

"Kelly's been asking to come too and the rest of her friends. I think Mum and Dad might agree now that Mrs Baxter's spoken to them. She said the girls really needed to see Jess."

"Thanks, Mrs Baxter," I said in my head. "I owe you. I just wish you'd said something before."

"I bet Jess really wants to have them here too," Will said.

"Yes, yes, yes," my brain called out. I *do*. If only my parents had listened to him, if only Mrs Baxter had intervened earlier, my friends might have been able to sit around my bed and entertain me. Maybe they'd have been able to pull me back from the brink and I'd never have got to this stage, but then I'd never have been through the last few days, never learned all of those lessons in living. Sometimes, some things are meant to be.

Will sat back in the chair and I knew that he was looking down at me.

"I'd have been before, you know," he said softly. I knew he was talking to Jamie but it felt as if he was saying it to me too. "But obviously your parents do what they think is right. I really want to help, any way I can. If you want someone to come and sit with her, I'm more than happy."

"Thanks for the teddy bear," Jamie said. "Jess would love that, especially if she knew it was from you."

"You think?" Will asked.

"Of course," my brother replied. "She's always

had a bit of a thing for you. I thought you knew that."

So Jamie did know how I felt after all. I wondered what Will was doing now, what he was thinking. Was he blushing like me?

"I'm quite into her too," Will murmured.

I felt the air part as he leaned towards me.

"Bye, Jess," he murmured. "See you soon."

Then, before I had the chance to register what was happening, he had dusted my forehead with the lightest of kisses, right in front of my brother. His breath was cool and fresh, like the seaside on a beautiful, breezy day. It was awesome.

I'd waited my whole life for a moment like that. I wanted to reach out with my arms, to touch those fingers that were irresistibly close to mine. I tried so hard to move my hand. "Move, will you, move," I instructed my joints, my muscles, my tendons. "This is the first and last opportunity you've got to touch him, to feel the warmth of his skin next to yours."

I concentrated really hard and imagined the messages travelling from my brain to my fingers.

I almost felt as if my arm was extending and contacting with the slight sandpaper-dryness of his fingertips as they met mine.

"Oh my God!" Will leapt up, almost pushing the chair over. "She moved! She touched my hand!"

His shoes squeaked slightly on the floor as he spun around.

"I didn't imagine it, did I?" Will shouted.

I'd already heard Jamie spring from the window sill. He banged into the bed and I knew that they were both looking down at me.

"No," he said, "you didn't imagine it. I saw it too."

My brother leaned in closer.

"Jess, it's me, Jamie. Can you hear me? Wiggle your finger if you can hear me."

I concentrated hard again and felt my middle finger move.

"Stay there," Jamie said, presumably to Will, because I wasn't going anywhere. "I'm going to find a nurse."

I wanted to grab hold of him, to tell him not to bother. It was pointless. So I'd moved my hand slightly. It didn't mean anything.

I was still going to die.

Will sank on to the bed and for a few blissful seconds we were totally on our own together.

"Welcome back, Jess," he said and he picked up my hand, cradling it in his. "I always knew you could do it. Remember when I accidentally kicked a football in your face when you were about four? Most girls would have cried their eyes out, but not you. You're tough, Jess, and beautiful, and we all love you so much. When you're out of here, perhaps we could go for a coffee somewhere – just the two of us. I knew you'd come back to us. I don't know how, but I just knew it."

Wow! He'd called me beautiful, he'd asked me on a date and he'd said he loved me? Was that really what I heard, really what he meant? I felt like one of those evening primrose flowers which come up in Mum's herbaceous border every summer. They bloom in the evening and begin to wither almost as soon as they reach their peak.

I wish I could come back, Will.

Would he hear my message? Could I make my thoughts so strong that they would filter

341

through his elation at my minuscule movement?

But I can't. I've made my decision and I've got to stick to it. I'm sorry. If there was anything I could do to change things, I would. It's all decided and it's too late to change my mind now.

As I lay there, my emotions swirling through me like water going down a plughole, I felt a single tear slide out from the corner of my eye.

MIRACLES

TUESDAY, 7 MARCH – 9.04 P.M.

All hell broke loose after that. Someone was shining a torch in my eyes. Will was cast aside and I wanted him back. People were everywhere, leaning over me, prodding me, calling out my name, swarming around me like wasps round an orange. Irritating, annoying people, rumpling my covers and stealing my space. Why couldn't they leave me alone with Will so that I could dream about what might have been? You'd think I'd performed the so-called Miracle of the Moving Hand the amount of fuss they made – doctors and nurses coming backwards and forwards, babbling incessantly.

At least everyone was talking to me differently now, as if I was a real person once more, as if I could understand them, instead of saying things like 'How are we today, Jessica?' and obviously not expecting an answer. I tried to tell them all to be quiet, that I wanted to say goodbye in peace, that I'd done everything I could to stay with them but it was nearly time for me to leave. But they were talking at me, talking to each other. No one was listening properly, except for me. If they carried on like this I'd never be able to hear Darren calling me through the pandemonium, but maybe it wouldn't be like that this time. Maybe Death would be stealthy and silent, like a softly padding cat hunting a mouse, and it would all be over in an instant.

Mum rushed through the door beating herself up for slipping away to go to the loo and get a coffee and not being there to witness the so-called miracle of my hand moving.

"Jess, darling. Oh, Jess. It's me, Mum."

I know Mum. Don't worry. I haven't forgotten who you are. I'd never do that.

"Can you move your hand again, Jess?" asked a doctor.

Yes, yes, okay. If I have to.

"Good girl," someone else said as my finger did a little wave. "That's wonderful."

No it isn't, I wanted to say. *Don't get your hopes up.* But it was no good. I could hear the optimism in their voices and feel the room filling up with joy. It made me feel so guilty. I shouldn't have tried to touch Will. I shouldn't have shown the rest of them what I could do. All I'd done was make things worse for everyone.

I had no idea what time it was but I knew it must be getting late. Someone had obviously called Dad because he'd arrived in the middle of all the confusion. Even Gran had left her bridge session and raced to the hospital. I half expected Great Uncle Peter to turn up, and he'd emigrated to New Zealand over thirty years ago.

"She's coming back to us," Mum said, as she stroked my forehead.

"I told you she would," Dad replied. "She's a real fighter, our Jess. Always has been."

For goodness' sake, Dad! All the excitement has gone to your head. I'm not a fighter at all. I'm a wimp. Dying is probably going to be the first thing in my entire life that I follow through to the end. You know how I lose heart and give up three-quarters of the way through a task. It infuriates you. Have you forgotten what I'm really like so soon? Have you begun to turn me into something I'm not, before I've even gone?

He pressed his face to mine. I smelled his after-shave balm. It reminded me of summer holidays, blissful days in our past.

"I'm here, Jess. I love you, sweetheart. We're going to be a proper family again. I'm so sorry for everything." His voice broke.

I heard the giant bubble of emotion burst in his chest. I tried to turn, to press my skin closer to his, to ease his heartache.

It's okay, Dad. I love you too. Perhaps I didn't show how much I love you. Perhaps none of us did. If we all took you for granted, I'm sorry. I wish I could make it all right for us. I really do.

Tick, tick, tick went the clock as Dad's heartbeat tuned in with mine. I wanted to put my arms around him, to let him know that I forgave him, to let him know that I'd learned a lot in the last few days. I wanted him to know that I understood that grown-ups couldn't behave like grown-ups all the time, even if children expected them to. That it was just too much to ask. Sometimes we have to become adults before we're ready, like Kelly, and sometimes we have to make mistakes to find out how to make things right.

You're lucky, Dad. I felt the words float out of me. *Mum still loves you. She'll always love you. You've got a second chance, a chance to sort things out. Don't blow it.*

He sobbed into my pillow, his face against my hair, huge, racking sobs that rocked the bed and shook the room. I sensed Mum and Jamie bend over, their arms wrapping both him and me in a protective cocoon. We stayed like that, merged into a tender heap and I felt the tendrils of family wind around me like those sweet peas clinging to their canes. We were family. We would always be bound together.

Eventually Gran left and Dad took Jamie home. It was just Mum and me. I tried to open my eyes slightly to see through a lattice of eyelashes. Despite the exhausted slackness of her skin, Mum's eyes were suddenly brighter. In those hazel kaleidoscopes I saw her belief in my recovery, and a burning pain shot through my heart.

Was this it, the end? Was it going to be early?

 347

Surely it couldn't be after midnight already? Suddenly there was so much still left to say, so many things I wanted to ask. I tried to say it all in my head, to concentrate on the words and not the pain in my chest which had turned to a dull ache.

I'm sorry, Mum! I wish I'd been a better daughter. I wish I'd helped around the house more and kept my bedroom tidier and made you cups of tea when you'd been working in the garden. I wish I hadn't sulked when you wouldn't let me have my ears pierced, or broken your favourite Christmas tree ornament because I was in too much of a hurry to get it out of the box. I wish I'd realised, Mum, before it was too late, how much better I could be at everything if I put my mind to it.

She lifted my hand and pressed it against her cheek.

I'd be a better sister, too, and a better friend. Kelly's a really nice person and I'm so glad she and Jamie are together. She'll look after him. She'll look out for Nat and Yasmin, too. I forgot to write in your diary that it's Nat's birthday next week. Please don't arrange my funeral for then, Mum. Things aren't always what you expect, are they, Mum? I've found out so much and I wish that we could sit down on the sofa at home to talk it through. I wish you could put your arm around me and I could rest my head on your shoulder while we watch a rom-com together.

She was playing with my fingers. I could feel the slight snag at the edge of one of her nails. I wished I could file it down, smooth the edges, massage cream into her hands the way she'd done with mine.

"Mrs Baxter rang me," Mum said. "I know you've never got on with her but she wants what's best for you, Jess. She asked if your friends could come and see you for a short time. She thinks it would do them good. Perhaps I should have let them come before but I didn't want them to be upset. Would it be a good idea now? Perhaps not everyone at once – that would be too much. Maybe just Sara to start with. Would you like her to pop in on Saturday, sweetheart?"

Oh Mum, I won't be here by then. And, if I was, I'm not sure that I'd want to see her. She's hurt me, Mum. You'd probably tell me to forgive her. You'd probably say that grief affects people in all sorts of funny ways and that she wouldn't have made a play for Will if she hadn't been so upset about my accident.

You'd tell me that true friends love unconditionally, and that forgiving someone doesn't mean condoning what they've done. But you're so kind, Mum, you think well of everyone, you're always there for us. I wish I could have always been there for you. I wish I could be as kind as you, but I'm not and I don't know if I want to see Sara again. Is that right, Mum? What do you think?

I felt the room light up as she smiled at me.

"I think everything's going to turn out just fine," Mum said, as she traced her finger around my face.

Oh Mum! I thought. *How wrong can you be?*

The hospital was quietening down and it had to be getting really late.

"I'm going now, sweetheart," Mum whispered. "I'll be back first thing in the morning."

She kissed me. She had brought me into this world and it seemed right that her devoted kiss was entrusting me to the next. I wondered if she could hear *my* heart breaking now?

Bye, Mum, I breathed. *Don't ever forget how much I love you. I'll always love you, wherever I am and wherever you are.*

At last I was alone. The lights were low and it had to be close now – perhaps less than an hour away.

I lay listening and waiting. I felt quite calm until a soft, glowing light came towards me.

Not another pain of a doctor, I thought. If anyone else shines another torch in my eyes I'll tell them what I really think.

"Don't blame you, pet."

That wasn't a doctor or Darren. I wanted to see properly. I struggled with my eyelids. Who would have thought something so delicate could be so weighty, but I did it. I opened my eyes halfway. Someone was standing by the window.

"Gramps!" I said. "What are you doing here? Have you come to fetch me? That's so lovely."

He stepped to the side and curled his hands around the metal rail at the bottom of the bed.

"Jessica, sweetheart," he said in that soft, billowy voice which I missed so much, "it's time to say goodbye."

"Oh, is Darren going to call me now?"

Gramps moved closer. Minty breath chased up my nostrils and down my throat.

"I've got some good news for you." He sat on the edge of my bed. "It's not time yet."

"I don't understand. What do you mean? I'm on the list. I have to die."

"No, Jess, you don't. You're going to live."

"But that's impossible. Darren said it had to be me or Sara and I told him…"

Horror flowed through me.

"He hasn't…"

"No, no, no," Gramps reassured. "Sara's fine. Darren doesn't have a list any more."

I frowned, and felt the scar at the back of my head contract.

"Why not? What's happened to him?"

"Darren's no longer an angel of death. He's resigned and passed his list over to someone else, but before he did that he deleted your name."

Gramps smiled.

"I think Darren became rather fond of you. He wanted me to thank you, Jess. You helped him to realise that he can't spend an eternity trying to do something he's not cut out for. He wants more time to himself so he can come back and visit his gran."

"Oh!"

I tried to take it in. Was it really true? Where were the sounds of champagne corks popping, the jubilant singing, the whoops of triumph, all of those things that you imagine at times of celebration? I looked at Gramps and wondered if he was like a mirage, as if it was a last parting trick of the mortal world, or maybe he was really here, being kind, distracting me to dilute the fear.

"It *is* true, Jess." Gramps had read my thoughts. "You've got a wonderful life ahead of you."

"I can't believe it. It's like a miracle. Why? Why me? What have I done to deserve it?"

He caressed my cheek with his palm. It felt like being bathed in sunshine.

"Miracles do happen, Jess. Remember I said to you that visiting your friends could be more important than you realised? Well, I've been watching you. I've seen you learning and taking strength from your visits. I've seen you find a courage which you didn't know you had. You *are* a fighter, my darling girl. Promise me that you'll never stop fighting for what you believe in."

"I promise."

I stretched out my hand. It was a little easier now. Gramps brought his hand down to touch mine and happiness flowed through our fingers.

"I wish you could stay with me."

Gramps smiled but his eyes turned watery.

"When I've gone from sight, Jess, it doesn't mean that I'm not there."

His voice was getting softer. It was so quiet that I had to strain to catch the end of the sentence.

"We're still together, Jess, in here."

He touched his heart.

"Everything you do and everything you say contains a memory of me."

He stood up.

"It's not enough." I was crying now, trying to reach out to him, but he had moved away, as bright as the stars and as unreachable.

"Shhh," he hushed. "I know it isn't, but it's all we've got. So try to make it enough, Jess. Try to remember that I'm always with you, always watching over you."

"Like a guardian angel?"

"Yes, a bit like a guardian angel."

He shimmered through my tears.

"If you see Darren, tell him I'm happy for him, happy that he's going to spend time with his gran."

"I will. Will you do something for me?"

"You know I will. Anything."

"Look after *your* gran for me?" he asked. "Go and prick out a few seeds with her while you're recuperating. She'll like that."

"So will I. I'll like it a lot."

Gramps was fading fast now.

"I love you, Gramps. Stay with me," I begged, "just a little bit longer."

"I told you, poppet, I'm always with you. Don't you forget that."

"I'll try not to. I promise."

And my gramps completely disappeared into the dimness.

Midnight came and went. It was Wednesday the eighth of March. The seconds ticked down.

Nothing happened. 00.02. I was still alive.

Love

Three weeks later I was home. The doctors were stunned by my powers of recovery. They said it was because I was young and fit, but I still had the feeling that they were a bit bemused, that only a short time before they had written me off. Unlike my friends and family: they never gave up on me.

I had so many people wanting to visit me in hospital that Mum had to draw up a rota. Sara, Kelly, Nat and Yasmin were top of the list. I wasn't sure about seeing Sara, and she obviously wasn't totally sure about seeing me either because she was quiet, wary even, on that first visit to the hospital, although she'd got absolutely no idea that I knew about her and Will. I didn't want to hold a grudge. I wanted to be generous and forgiving. I'd been given a second chance. It seemed only fair that she should have one too. In reality, it wasn't that simple. We were so awkward with each other, and I couldn't see how we'd ever get back to being the good friends we were before.

My speech was still a bit slow and I was weak and tired, but physically everything else was pretty much back to normal. I wanted to return to school but everyone said that I mustn't rush things, so I'm only going in for the odd lesson and Mrs Baxter comes to the house once a week to give me maths tuition. If the weather's nice, we sit in the garden and drink tea and eat biscuits while we work through the exercises she has set me. I can't say that I'll ever enjoy maths but I don't hate it nearly as much as I used to. Now when Mrs Baxter tells me that I don't know what I'm capable of until I really try, I don't dismiss it. I listen to her and I believe.

I won't be back at school properly until September, which gives me a lot of time to think. I think of my life in the past and my life in the future. I think about my home and my family, those on earth and in heaven. I think about Will and how much we have to look forward to together. I have realised the true meaning of the saying 'live every day as if it is your last' and I have made a promise to myself: that I will try to be a better person than I was before. Of course, I know that sometimes I will fail but that doesn't matter. It's the trying that counts, and I know that I can fight back, pick myself up from my mistakes and learn from them. The backward steps will be there to help me relish the forward ones. I may even learn to love Will's dog.

Before the accident I'd never felt lucky, but now each day is a gift. Even the bad days, when I am tired and crotchety, I always find something to be glad about, whether it's Mum's efforts to be a better cook as she stuffs me with endless fruit and veg recipes, or one of Dad's gentle strolls across the fields to build up my stamina.

One of the best things is having Dad properly back in my life. The affair is over, or so he says. He says that he wants us to be a proper family again and we're trying. It's not easy, and I still don't really trust him. Mum doesn't either. I've caught her checking his phone and she always wants to know where he's been, who he's been with. But we're all doing our best and, as Gran says, that's all you can do. We're not perfect but we are kinder to one another. Jamie doesn't complain when I ask him to remove a spider from my room and he even remembers to make me the odd cup of tea, although adding sugar to it seems to be beyond him.

He was a bit perplexed about my funeral note. It was about ten o'clock at night and I was lying in bed writing my diary when he came through to my room. He was holding his hands behind his back.

"Jess, I found this in one of my cricket books."

He produced the note.

"How did it get there?"

I had to think fast. There was no alternative. I had to lie.

"Oh that! I put it there just before the accident. Isn't it odd, as if I had a premonition or something?"

He frowned.

"I'm sure I'd have seen it."

I shrugged, yawned.

"It's amazing what we miss when it's right in front of us."

 359

"Yeah," he muttered. "I suppose you're right. All the same..."

He stared down at the piece of paper.

"Jamie," I said, "throw it away. Please. It makes me feel weird."

He shuddered.

"I know what you mean. Me too."

He screwed it up and threw it in the bin.

"You know what *was* weird?"

I felt my heart skip a beat.

"What?"

He looked around my room.

"When you were in the coma, those last few days before you started to come round – once or twice I thought you'd been here, in this room."

"Now, that *is* weird," I said.

I wanted to tell him. I really did. But I couldn't. I couldn't tell anyone what had happened to me. They'd never believe it. To be honest, it's only been a few weeks and I'm beginning to wonder if I believe it myself. That's why I took that funeral note out of the bin after Jamie had crumpled it up. I flattened it out and placed it in my diary to remind me that it was real, it did happen and that I really am lucky, probably the luckiest girl in the world.

I've spent a lot of time with Gran. We've planted cosmos and marigolds and beetroot seeds. I'm not a fan of beetroot but Gran says it's really good for your energy levels so I suppose I'll give it another try when it's ready to eat. We've sorted out a big box of loose photos and put them in albums with little captions underneath. There were a lot of pictures of Gramps in there and I've kept a couple to put on the pinboard in my room. In one of them I am standing under the walnut tree in our garden and Gramps has his arm around my shoulder.

To look at me now, I am pretty much the same Jessica I was then, a bit taller but I have the same straight brown hair, same grey/green eyes and smattering of freckles across my cheeks. But that's not the truth. Underneath I am different, and if I have learned one thing from this experience it is the importance of looking beneath the surface.

When I'm well enough, I want to go and look for the tramp in the park and do something for one of the homeless charities because I know what it's like to feel that you don't belong anywhere, not to know where you're going to sleep at night. Now, when I go to sleep, safe in my own bed, I give thanks that I have another life to live. I made a promise to myself and to everyone who was there for me when I was in my coma that I will not waste it. It's a promise I intend to keep.

Kelly threw that party for me and it was one of the happiest nights of my life so far. I didn't manage to wear the pink top I'd seen in the shops that day when I was following Sara because they'd sold out, but Mum bought me a new dress instead and took me to the nail bar. I chose a deep purple polish and the technician applied tiny pale pink hearts to the tips. I'd had layers put through my hair to hide the shorter bits which were taking time to grow back, and I felt really grown-up and glamorous as I walked up to Kelly's front door.

It was a warm evening and there were fairy lights and candles strewn all around the garden. Even though it was just the five of us, we had loads of food, balloons and a three-tiered chocolate cake decorated with crystallised violets. Nat put crisps *and* cheese-and-tomato sandwiches on her plate. She even ate a slim slice of cake although she did leave a bit of the icing. Kelly's dad seemed to genuinely smile as he hustled the boys out of the front door on their way to the cinema and on the window sill in the kitchen was Kelly's latest tennis trophy. Yas even brought her sketchbook with her and did a quick drawing of us all sitting on the picnic rug in the middle of the lawn. I knew that she wouldn't have confronted her parents and told them that she didn't really want to be a doctor, but at least if she ever does reach that stage I will be here to support her.

I was sitting on the swing seat when Sara sidled up to me. She'd been subdued, and had kept her distance all evening. She placed a parcel on my lap. It was wrapped in indigo tissue paper and tied with a wide pink satin ribbon.

"What's this?" I asked.

"I made it for you when you were in hospital."

She sounded nervous, and wouldn't look me in the eye.

 363

"If you don't like it you can say so."

I tore off the paper. Inside was the blue cushion she had been working on when I'd visited her house. Across the front, it was appliquéd with a beautiful rainbow.

"I know that you've always liked rainbows."

I nodded, feeling a tightness in my chest.

"It's lovely. Thank you."

Clumsily I hugged her and she began to cry.

"Jess, there's something I want to tell you. I've done something awful. Kelly wasn't going to ask me to come tonight and I don't blame her."

I pressed the cushion to me, felt the tightness ease.

"I wanted you here, Sara."

Instinctively I reached out and stroked her arm.

"You know, don't you?" she said, tears streaming down her cheeks. "I didn't mean to do it. I just don't know what came over me. You were so ill and I wasn't allowed to see you and when I thought about you no longer being here..."

She started to sob.

"You must hate me, Jess."

"Of course I don't hate you."

I leaned over and put my arms around her.

"We all make mistakes," I murmured.

"Who told you?" she asked, holding tight, her tears trickling on to my shoulder.

I eased away, looked straight at her, forcing her to look back at me.

"It doesn't matter. What matters is that I'm here now with all of you."

She sniffed and glanced over at the others who were sorting out some music.

"Things will never be the same again though, will they? There's an atmosphere. They're doing their best but you must be able to sense it. They'll never forgive me."

It was then that I knew I had to let it go, to put it behind me, for all our sakes. I took her hand, knelt down on the grass and beckoned to Kelly, Nat and Yasmin.

"Of course they'll forgive you. If I can, so can they."

I looked from one to the other and gestured for everyone to link hands and form a circle. They did it, with a hint of reluctance.

"Once upon a time we said we'd be friends for life. Do you remember that?" I asked.

They nodded.

"Well," I took a deep breath, "that's what I want more than anything."

We were all crying now. I looked at my friends who had helped me in more ways than they would ever know.

"Can you do that, for me? Please?"

Kelly, Nat and Yasmin nodded.

"They're only saying that because you're here," Sara murmured.

I squeezed her hand.

"Maybe it'll take them a bit of time," I said, smiling at everyone before returning my gaze to Sara. "But do you know what?"

"What?" she asked.

"Time," I replied, "is something we have plenty of."

She nodded and smiled back.

And at that very moment a feather floated down and landed right in the middle of our circle.

"My mum says that means there's an angel

passing overhead," Nat chuckled.

"Yeah, right!" Kelly scoffed. "Who believes in angels? I think an owl is more likely."

I picked up the feather and held it to the light. Its silver edge sparkled in the glow from one of the candles.

"I believe in angels," I said softly, as I looked up at the star-strewn sky, "and this is definitely an angel feather. Trust me."